RUNNING WITH A DOPE BOY'S HEART

An African American Urban Standalone

LAKIA

Published by Lakia Presents, LLC.

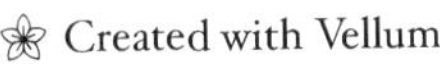

JOIN AUTHOR LAKIA'S MAILING LIST!

To stay up to date on new releases, contests, and sneak peeks join my mailing list. Subscribers will enjoy the FIRST look at all content from Author Lakia plus exclusive short stories!
https://bit.ly/2RTP3EV

JACKSON "JAX" RICHMOND

Taking a pull from the blunt, I allowed the weed to permeate my lungs in an attempt to ease my mind before slowly exhaling. *Homebody* by Rob49 sounded off in the strip club and the hoes in our section went crazy. I passed the blunt to Blane as he tossed ones in the air. Pulling the rubber band off a fresh band of ones, I was prepared to stand and toss out some cash until I felt a soft body plop down in my lap without my permission.

Gripping the bitch by her neck, I forced her ass up out of my lap and back to her feet. Standing with her neck in my left hand and the band of ones in the right, I ensured that she didn't bust her ass in the eight inch heels. I didn't give a fuck that she was laced with an enticing fragrance and the softest skin. You needed consent to invade my personal space, I didn't play that shit, even if we were in a strip club. Although I was vibing, my eyes were locked on the entrance in case something popped off and she was obstructing my view.

"Jax, let me go," Dior's squeaky ass voice called out.

"This why I don't brang my ass in here because you always with some bullshit," I vexed, releasing her.

"You know I like getting you all riled up then calming you down," she licked her juicy lips.

This bitch was crazy as fuck, she loved playing with a deadly nigga and I kept filling her up with dick, so I was no better. Slipping the band of money in Dior's hand, I leaned in to whisper in her ear. "I'mma come find you before I slide but you know Ion like hoes being all on me in here so chill."

"Okay daddy," she cooed, stuffing the money into the drawstring bag she had dangling from her wrist. She stared into my eyes like she loved me or some shit, making me uncomfortable as fuck. All that hoe loved was money. That's all these bitches in here really wanted from a nigga.

"And get one of your friends to slide with us. Preferably that flexible bitch," I encouraged, slapping Dior's fat ass.

She winked and finally moved the fuck around. I went to grab another band of money from the table to throw out when one of my phones vibrated in my pocket. Pulling them out, I confirmed it was my trap phone with a text from Maleek.

Capo: That nigga Madden got people posted up here. (maps attachment) Handle that and Madden.

Me: Sliding.

Slipping the phone back in my pocket, I snatched the stripper out of Blane's lap. "Aye get the fuck on."

The woman stared up at me with fearful eyes until I passed her the new stack of ones in my hand. Her timid frown turned into an excited grin as she strutted over to another nigga from our crew.

"The fuck you doing Jax?"

"We got some shit to handle, you driving," I commanded.

He nodded in understanding before following me out of the section. We hopped in our whips and went to an abandoned lot where a 1995 Camry was waiting with the key underneath the seat. This was a duty we routinely performed, eliminating the need for words. Blane took the driver's seat and I slid into the passenger before he took off.

"Who spot this is?' Blane broke the silence as we sat idle watching the residence in question.

"Maleek said some of Madden's niggas setup shop here. I'mma go see that nigga once we finish here."

Dressed in all black with the ski mask concealing my identity, I glanced at the two Glocks with switches and extended clips in my lap, then back up at the trap house in the middle of the hood. The street-lights were out and the dark street offered a great cloak for my madness. Besides the raucous crickets in the distance, there wasn't anyone else out here which left me even more baffled. These niggas didn't have no motion, so I racked my brain attempting to understand why the fuck they decided to go against the grain, and lay their life on the line for pennies. You'd think after all of these years and bodies, my name and reputation would proceed itself in Birmingham and the next city over, but I loved when niggas decided to gamble and step out of line.

The lights inside of the living room shut off and the front door swung open. Two niggas stepped out, one passing a blunt to the other, oblivious to their grim reality. Silently nodding my head, Blane placed his foot on the gas and I stuck the upper half of my body out of the window and let my guns spit. The clip was empty and both men laid motionless drenched in crimson within the matter of a minute. Blane spun the whip around at the end of the block giving me time to replace the clips. When we passed the house I let my guns rip the property to shreds as the tires squealed heading down the block. Easing back into my seat, I lit the blunt as the cold wind greeted me from the lowered window.

"Come on nigga, let that window up, it's cold as fuck out there." Blane bitched and I ignored his ass just as I do these nagging ass hoes.

The cold air slapping my face was soothing in that moment and I soaked it up until we pulled into the abandoned lot and hopped out of the whip. Blane retrieved a gas can from the trunk of the parked car and dumped it on the incriminating evidence before sending it up in smoke. Blane stood by, teeth chattering, while I finished off my blunt and tossed the roach into the burning car along with my ski mask before hopping into my own truck.

Blane motioned for me to roll my window down and I obliged, annoyed as fuck. When it was time to put in work I preferred silence so I could focus on every detail. A simple mistake could be the difference between a prison cell and my memory foam pillow top mattress. "You sure you don't want me to slide with you?"

"I'm straight," I waved that nigga off.

In addition to silence, I preferred to do shit solo, I'd never snitch on myself. Blane was trustworthy but I didn't put shit past anybody besides Maleek, that's the only man that I felt would never betray me. I mashed on the gas, pulling away from Blane and the burning vehicle before somebody called the police.

When I made it to the hole in the wall bar in Bessemer, the two men, clad in all black like myself, in front of the door immediately took notice of my young ass when I stepped out of my truck with my hood up. It seemed like I was always out of place, most men playing the position I was in were well into their thirties, while I was a young twenty-four year old making waves in their pond. The large age gap didn't mean shit to me, my mentor molded me into the man I am today. Plus I put in work and earned my seat at the table, so these niggas with their menacing glares didn't strike an ounce of fear in me.

"The fuck you doing 'round these parts? Yo young ass can't get in? It's twenty-five and up, you ain't make the cut." The big nigga guarding the door chuckled with his arms folded across his chest and his partner beside him joined in on the laughter. Pulling my nine from my waist, I gripped his shirt and stuck it beneath his chin before anyone else could react. His hands were in the air and his partner's eyes looked like they were about to bulge from his head.

"Aye young bull chill, we just trying to do our job and make it home to our families," his giggly ass partner pleaded for this nigga. My grimace met his face momentarily and he stepped back. I pulled the hoody off my head, exposing my face and these niggas looked like they saw a ghost once my identity was revealed.

"I'm only twenty-four and the last place I wanna be is outside of this shit hole y'all call a bar in this dusty ass city with a bunch of old country hoes. Mr. Giggles, go grab Madden. You got ten seconds and if you ain't back I'mma blow this nigga's head off and shoot this shit up to draw him out," I monotoned.

The door swung open and the security guard ran into Madden's chest he was moving so fucking fast. "Chill J... J... Jax, this isn't necessary, let me explain. I already got word..."

I shoved the shaking security guard off to the side and he took off running as I waved my hand in front of my throat signaling for Madden to shut his stuttering ass up. The sound of footsteps approaching caused Madden to raise his hand. I shrugged my shoulders and turned around to face the four men that came to Madden's defense. A twinge of guilt consumed me as I came face to face with the young niggas Madden had running with him, then a sly grin spread across my face. It was time to shake some shit up with these young niggas who Madden clearly felt were expendable.

"Jax, put the gun down and let's talk this shit out inside," Madden urged.

"Nah, I think yo lil team should know what you got going on," I nodded my head, looking at his slim ass team that was positioned on the uncut grass that led up to the bar.

"I came here to put a bullet in Madden's head then lay the rest of his team down because we learned that he had the audacity to step into Birmingham territory instead of doing his thing in Bessemer like he been doing for years. He sent two of y'all people into our city like sacrificial lambs. Everybody know that Jax and Maleek got Birmingham on lock, we don't give a fuck about what y'all do on y'all turf just don't step on our shit and you won't get stepped on."

"Come on Jax, that area was unoccupied and it was right on the edge of the city."

At the sound of Madden's voice, I lifted my nine and whacked him across the head. He leaned over in pain, ears probably ringing like a motha fucka, and I pressed my gun to the back of his head while he held the side of his head. "Shut the fuck up!" I silenced Madden before refocusing on the men before me. "Like I was saying, y'all all look young and impressionable so I'm thinking Madden left y'all in the dark about what was going on. I been in this game long enough to know how these old heads can do the young niggas."

"And that was my lil brother he put at that trap house!" One of the men from the grass stepped up, pulling his gun and aiming it at Madden with tears threatening to fall from his eyes.

"Pull that trigger and Bessemer is yours," I shrugged.

Without a second thought, the young bull pulled the trigger and Madden's body tumbled to the ground. I stepped over his corpse and the men parted, making a path for me. Halfway down the walkway, I lifted my gun and sent a bullet through the temple of the young bull who murdered Madden. His body plopped to the ground next and Madden's other four men jumped back. The devil and angel on my shoulder had a brief debate with each step I took towards my truck. I wanted to spare the lil nigga, but I couldn't have him coming back on me later seeking revenge for his brother's death. Unfortunately, it was no secret that I would lay anybody down who stepped into our territory. He didn't hesitate to body Madden, that was a young shooter in the making and I would be a fool to allow that type of nigga to walk around with an ax to grind. Although I decided to give everyone else a second chance, he wouldn't have the same opportunity.

"I guess whoever cleans this shit up is in charge," I shrugged. "I'll make sure the product finds y'all."

Hopping in my black Dodge Durango SRT Hellcat, I watched as the light skinned nigga with a mouth full of gold teeth took charge, ordering them niggas around while hopping on a flip phone. He was next up for sure. I pulled off and parked a street over next to an abandoned house where I had a clear view of the chaos I left in front of the bar. I wasn't worried about witnesses because the bar was a front for Madden's stash and the houses surrounding the area were abandoned. While I watched the scene unfold I placed a call to Maleek and that shit went unanswered. It was close to one o'clock in the morning, so I'm sure his ass was asleep by now. My decision to let these niggas live would have to stand, and we'd discuss the shit in the morning. Especially since I had two strippers ready to take turns gargling my dick for the rest of the night.

KODA ALLEN

"Would you like a bacon wrapped scallop, Ms. Allen?"

I glanced at the appetizers placed on the silver serving platter and my stomach churned. The food looked delectable; Maleek's restaurant was catering the event, so I knew the food was good. Unfortunately, I didn't feel well. If I could've skipped this event, I would have, but Maleek insisted that it wouldn't be a good look if his fiancée wasn't on his arm. Yet, I hadn't spotted his face in the last thirty minutes. I'm sure he was skinning and grinning in one of these rich white men's face, while I stood here in these heels that were killing my feet, ready to go home.

"No thank you."

Shaking my head, I declined the beautiful woman's offer and she went on her way, offering the hors-d'oeuvres to other patrons at this stuffy ass event. We were attending a mixer for entrepreneurs in Birmingham and I would've much rather been anywhere else. The butler passed hors d'oeuvres style events were usually my favorite type of events; I didn't have to sit at a table and pretend to engage in elitist conversations. The space was beautifully decorated and the menu was on point, but I wasn't in the mood to pretend tonight. We were one of a handful of minorities in the building and that always came along with microaggressions and slips of racist tongues. I don't know how Maleek could do it, but he ignored the shit with ease to achieve his goals. Unfortunately, it seemed like these were the only type of events we attended lately. I wanted to do something fun for a change and if I couldn't do that, I at least wanted to rest in my bed when I didn't feel one hundred percent.

Taking a swig from my champagne flute, I decided I had enough of the bland conversations and fake smiles with all of these uppity motha fuckas. Another server carrying champagne passed by and I stopped him to exchange my empty flute before exiting the ballroom. Making my way to the hallway, I plopped my Airpods in my ear and opened the HBO app to watch the new episode of *Rap Shit* that this event made me miss.

Ten minutes into the episode, I sensed a pull on the long-sleeve gown Maleek had picked out for me, designed to conceal my tattoos, which, according to him, weren't a good look. Twirling around, I faced Maleek's menacing glare.

"The fuck is you doing?" He spat.

"I..."

"You know what fuck it. If you don't wanna be here that bad take yo ass home instead of standing out here playing on your phone like a fucking lil girl. Sometimes I think a woman my age may be better suited for this lifestyle. You don't appreciate a fucking thing," Maleek gritted in a low tone, but I felt the venom lacing each word. He was furious.

"Maleek, I..."

My words were cut short as Maleek stepped in my direction, sending trepidation through my body. "Take yo ass home before you piss me off." He requested, planting a kiss on my cheek before passing me the keys. "I got enough shit going on in the streets and in this event center. And pull the sleeve of your dress up, your trashy ass tattoos are showing," Maleek grumbled.

Doing as Maleek requested, I understood that further conversation would risk public humiliation. His demand wasn't out of the ordinary. Whenever Maleek had the opportunity, he never hesitated to express how he thought my tattoos made me look trashy. Two weeks ago on Christmas, Maleek gifted me prepaid laser tattoo removal sessions because he was determined to turn me into somebody I'm not. Now that we were twenty-six and thirty-five, that age gap was starting to show. I still wanted to live vivaciously and this nigga wanted to climb social ladders during the day, while poisoning the streets at night. This motha fucka clearly thought he was James St. Patrick.

Offering Maleek one final smirk, I clasped the keys in my grasp, and I strutted towards the exit with my head held high. Home was where I wanted to be anyways. I kicked the stilettos off once I was safely inside of Maleek's Porsche Cayenne and drove home relaxed and barefoot.

When I made it home, it was a little after ten o'clock. My stomach was still doing somersaults, I probably should've drank water instead of champagne, but I needed the depressant to fight through the bullshit that accompanied those types of events. After soaking in my garden tub until my fingertips pruned, I climbed into my bed with a bottle of ice cold water and finished watching the episode of *Rap Shit* before drifting to a deep sleep.

Maleek plopping in bed next to me interrupted my sleep. His rough hands rubbed up and down my leg, and I glanced at the time on my alarm clock and it was two o'clock in the morning. I wanted to ask his ass where the fuck he was for the past hour because the event ended at midnight but I didn't. Remaining still and silent, I prayed he would lay down and drift off to lala land so I didn't have to argue with his ass. That would've been too much like right because Maleek pulled me over to face him, forcing my eyes open.

"Come on Koda, get up and ride this dick," he demanded, tugging at the tie around his neck and pulling it over his head.

Admiring his side profile, I couldn't deny how handsome this man was. His cinnamon brown skin, thick brows, and colgate smile would have any woman in a trance. Dressed to impress at all times, he was a single bitch's kryptonite. The Armani suit, impeccably tailored to his form, drew attention to his muscular build. On an average day, I would rush to hop on his dick, but now that the queasy stomach subsided, I had a headache. Which I'm sure was due to lack of sleep.

"I still don't feel good, Maleek, and I have to go into the office for my monthly meeting in the morning," I explained.

"Man," he grumbled, hopping from the bed.

I heard his ass march out of the room but I was exhausted and allowed sleep to consume me again. When I woke up the next morning Maleek was in the shower getting ready for the day. Silencing the persistent alarm, I slid out of bed to do the same. After finishing my oral and skincare routine, I entered the kitchen to prepare breakfast.

The aroma from bacon sizzling in the cast iron skillet made my stomach rumble. With my stomach doing somersaults last night I opted out of dinner, and now I was feeling famished. It took me a little longer than usual to get myself together and start breakfast but the french toast and bacon all looked delectable cooking simultaneously on the glass top stove.

My AppleWatch notified me that it was time to leave the house if I wanted to make my staff meeting on time. A twinge of panic settled in the pit of my stomach because that meant Maleek would be coming downstairs at any moment to leave for the day. Maleek was my boyfriend of ten years, and sometimes he was a blessing, but he was often a curse.

The start of our relationship was no fairy tale, in fact it would be seen as a crime if we were honest about when the relationship started. I met Maleek when I was sixteen years old and he was twenty-five. He lived across the street from my best friend Simone and played basketball with her older brother Randal. One night I was rushing home because it was past curfew and me, and Simone got sucked into reading all hundred comments on a Facebook post of two girls from our high school going back and forth over the quarterback of the football team.

My mom called my phone and told me I had five minutes to get my ass home or I would be inside for the rest of the week. I high tailed it out of Simone's house just as it started raining, I wasn't trying to be cooped up in the house all week. My house was a five minute walk and I was sprinting in the rain when I suddenly slipped and busted my ass. Maleek pulled up beside me, hopped out of his whip and helped me off the ground. My hip was throbbing so he asked me if I wanted a ride. I'd seen him around Simone's house before and exchanged pleasantries on a few occasions so I hopped in, thankful that I would make it in before my mom's time limit.

Maleek didn't try anything on me during the ride home, he did give me his number and offered to give me a ride anytime I needed one and I happily accepted it, thinking he was being a gentleman. Now that I'm ten years removed from that time, I realize that Maleek wasn't shit because he wasted no time flirting and putting the moves on my underage ass. Maleek had me so smitten that my young ass was doing shit I had no business for him. We kept our shit under wraps until after my high school graduation. With Maleek being twenty-seven, nearly ten years older than me, my parents raised eyebrows over the age gap. They accused Maleek of courting me when I was underage, but we vehemently denied that shit, planting the first wedge in my relationship with my parents.

The Samsung twenty-eight inch security monitor mounted on the left wall of the kitchen notified me that there was motion in the driveway and thoughts of the past faded. Live security footage from the exterior of our home played and I spotted Jax's Durango pulling into the driveway behind my AMG. Jax was Maleek's protégé, and I've known him since the eighth grade when my parents bought their forever home in the same Atlanta neighborhood as him and Simone. He went to middle school and high school with me and Simone but he was two years younger than us. In high school, me and Simone were on the cheerleading team and Jax played for the JV football team so we shared space often.

Plus Jax spent a lot of time at Simone's house as well because his older brother Kenneth was friends with Maleek and Randal. When Kenneth was murdered, Jax dropped off the face of the earth for a while and I couldn't blame him. In the span of five years his mom and brother were murdered, and his dad was sentenced to life in prison for her murder.

Losing Kenneth changed Jax, he withdrew from school and disappeared. When he resurfaced a year later, the young boy that we knew from high school didn't exist. Jax returned a menacing sixteen year old that people knew not to fuck with.

Hard bottoms rapidly colliding with the stairs caught my attention because Maleek's to-go plate wasn't prepared yet.

"What the fuck you been doing all morning? You ain't dressed and breakfast ain't ready," Maleek greeted my back, and I closed my eyes to fight the fury that instantly brewed inside of me. No greeting or anything, just straight disrespect before eight o'clock in the morning. I took a deep breath while stirring the eggs around in the pan. I wasn't in the mood for his bullshit this morning. "Bitch, I know you fucking hear me!" Maleek roared and I released the grip on the spatula, prepared to walk away but he caught my hair before I could move fast enough. I felt a few of my coils being ripped from the follicle as Maleek pulled me back to face him. "I let you slide with all that attitude last night, talking about you ain't wanna fuck and shit, but now you wake up on that same shit and I been trying Koda but what the fuck. It's like you want me to beat yo ass!"

WAP!

Maleek cocked his free arm back and punched me in the face. My body would've tumbled to the ground with the force he hit me with but Maleek still had a tight grip on my hair. "Please Maleek," I sobbed, placing my hands out in a protective manner as he pulled me off the ground by my hair so we were eye level.

"Aye what the fuck wrong with you Maleek?!" Jax's snarl caused my eyes to dart in his direction as he rushed into the kitchen gripping Maleek's hand that held my hair. "Get the fuck off of her!" He demanded before my body plopped down on the floor. I immediately hopped up and stood between the men, my eye was throbbing and the familiar scene sent me back to the last time someone caught Maleek putting his hands on me and tried to intervene.

Every year on Christmas Eve we went to visit Maleek's parents in Atlanta and spent the week there. The day was filled with shopping, an evening service at his parent's church, then back to their house for dinner. We were at the dinner table, enjoying the catered Christmas Eve dinner with his parents. Maleek loved steak and lobster, so that's what we were having with a side of garlic mashed potatoes and asparagus. The table was quiet, I'm not sure if something was going on between Maleek and his parents but the normally heartfelt Christmas Eve dinner was filled with tension.

"It's been eight years now. We need to be hearing wedding bells and pregnancy announcements soon. What are you two waiting for?" Mr. Pierce questioned.

"I'm thinking marriage for our ten year anniversary in two years and then the kids will come right after that," Maleek responded.

The math wasn't mathing for me. I repeatedly expressed the need to remain kid free until I reached thirty. That would give me more time to nurture my business and grow it to the point that it would run smoothly without me in the office on a daily basis.

"I thought we discussed waiting until I turned thirty, to give my business time to thrive," I expressed, taking a slow sip from my wine.

Maleek's face instantly frowned up and the fork full of steak that he was driving towards his mouth ceased in front of his lips. Exhaling deeply, Maleek placed his fork down to refocus his attention on my fearful face. At that point in our relationship, Maleek only slipped up and put his hands on me once, and I forgave him because he was everything I wanted in a man prior to that evening. However, that same apoplectic look reappeared in his eyes after I expelled my thoughts.

"I already fucking warned you that I wasn't in the mood for your bullshit today," Maleek snapped, refocusing his attention on me. "You talking like you run shit between us. Whatever I say, goes around this motha fucka. You wouldn't be where the fuck you are in life if it wasn't for me! If I say you gone pop out a few kids tomorrow that's what we gone do!"

"Maleek, relax." His mother scolded him but I didn't have to look up to know that Maleek's eyes were burning a hole in the side of my head. I was his target and when he got like this I was his archnemesis and needed to keep my mouth shut.

"I was just..."

WAP!

"Shut the fuck up Koda!" Maleek yelled while slapping me. Before the taste of blood filled my mouth Maleek was yanking me up from the table by my neck. Mr. Pierce jumped up from his seat and rushed to our side of the table.

"What is wrong with you?" Mr. Pierce questioned, pulling Maleek away from me.

"Get the fuck off of me. You might let mom run you but nah, Koda don't run me," Maleek challenged his father, pulling me back towards him.

"Let her go!" Mr. Pierce demanded before eyeing me. "Is this a regular thing? Does he abuse you?" I didn't answer because I wasn't a liar but the truth was my painful secret. My eyes stared at the floor, unwilling to give Maleek additional fuel to add to his blazing fire. "Son, we didn't raise you like this. You should go to the hotel and cool off, let Koda stay here with us tonight."

"Fuck no, she's coming with me. Fuck I look like leaving her here so y'all can get into her head with that do better bullshit. Nah, that's why we don't come around like that. We good," Maleek spat and pulled me towards the door but Mr. Pierce stood in our path, and looked me directly in the eyes.

"Koda, do you feel safe leaving with Maleek? I won't let him take you."

Maleek's switch was flipped and he released the grip on my arm and swung on his father, sending him flying into the dining room table. Food spurted in all directions as Maleek initiated an assault on his father. Mr. Pierce fought back to protect himself but the seventy something year old man was no match for his much younger and healthier son. Me and Mrs. Pierce were shouting and trying to pull Maleek off of his father but we were no match for his strength.

"You could've just minded your business!" Maleek spat, fluffing out his shirt before snatching my hand and pulling me out of the door.

That was the last time we saw or spoke with his parents and it seemed like the abuse got worse once he cut his parents off. Eventually, the relationship with my entire family came to a halt as well because they repeatedly encouraged me to leave once they found out about the abuse and Maleek wasn't having that.

Now I stood in the middle of this kitchen, between my longtime friend Jax and my volatile boyfriend Maleek. Jax was my last life line outside of Simone, and the snarl on his face told me that he didn't approve of the things he just saw. I was petrified that Maleek would attack Jax in this kitchen for his attempt to save me. Jax was always known to be crazy so I knew they would be embroiled in a battle that I would be unable to stop.

"You lucky," Maleek sneered, running his hands down his face before exiting the kitchen. I heard him rushing up the stairs and embarrassment consumed me as Jax stared at me with concern.

"Yo that nigga be over here whooping yo ass on the regular?" Jax questioned, eyes locked on mine, forcing me to cower. Not because I was fearful of him, but I was terrified that Maleek would hear him. His venomous tone, the indignation displayed on his face and fury behind his eyes forced me to lie.

"Please Jax, I'm fine," I placed my index finger over my lip.

Jax swiped my finger away from my face and I noticed his lip twitching. His demeanor and tone of voice signaled that he wasn't afraid of Maleek, but I was petrified. I honestly felt like there wasn't a restraining order or human being alive that could keep me safe from Maleek. That was until I noticed the rage brewing in Jax's dark brown orbs. I've witnessed angry Jax in the past and the shit wasn't pretty but maybe I was mistaken, I had to be. There was no way that Jax would be willing to put their brotherhood on the line to intervene in our domestic situations when they shared a tight big brother, lil brother bond.

Taking a long deep breath, I ignored Jax's stare as I washed my hands, prepared to put Maleek's food into the to-go plate. Jax marched over to me, cupping my chin, forcing my wet hands away from the sink as he examined my face. The pain was bearable so I was praying that my light skin wasn't turning black and blue.

Disgust filled Jax's eyes and he released the grip on my face. Embarrassed, I stared down at the marble counters as I waited for him to chastise me, encourage me to leave Maleek or utter anything. Jax wasn't usually a quiet man so I was expecting an earful. Then the sound of Jax walking away from me shattered my heart because he was leaving and I'd be left alone with Maleek.

"Even if he never hit you before, one time should be enough for you to walk the fuck away. You deserve better than that. I'll stay here while you pack your shit and..."

"No, I don't want to put you in the middle of our issues Jax." I stated in a low tone, ceasing his statement while my eyes remained fixated on the gray lines sprawled across the counter.

Jax's footsteps resumed momentarily followed by the front door slamming shortly afterwards. My eyes darted in the direction of the Echo Show and I saw Jax's Durango swerving out of our circular driveway fast as hell. Clearly he came over here to speak with Maleek, that was a regular occurrence for him. Like I mentioned before, Maleek was like Jax's older brother, he stepped up and helped raise him after his brother was murdered. Whatever brought Jax over here couldn't have been that important since he left without speaking to Maleek. If Jax wasn't so close to Maleek, I probably would've taken him up on his offer and packed my shit while he was here. Mentally and emotionally, I was over this relationship with Maleek. I felt like this for a while and I was putting shit in motion to get away from him. I just had one piece of the puzzle to put in place and I was going to disappear on his no good ass.

I finally turned the water off in the kitchen sink and quickly prepared Maleek's plate and sat it on the counter next to a bottle of Core water. Fighting my tears, I prepared a bag of ice for my eye and snuck my way up the stairs. Thankfully Maleek was in his office so I was free to get dressed in my bedroom. When I heard Maleek descend the stairs, I finally relaxed, thankful that he wouldn't attempt to finish the argument or assault today.

My appetite dissipated, I felt sluggish and now my eye was throbbing. Although I wasn't left with any visible marks from the assault, I was taking the day off. Once I watched Maleek's Range Rover pull out of the driveway, I climbed back into bed with my MacBook and opened my gmail account. The best part about being your own boss, you could make your own schedule and today I chose to work from home.

Although my romantic life was in fucking shambles, I was the proud owner of Stellar Financial Services where we specialized in investing, retirement and taxes. Since I can remember, I loved completing sudoku puzzles and other math activities. When we got our first computer I was a beast at playing minesweeper. It was my reward after completing all of my homework everyday and I loved every second of it. When I was bored, I enjoyed making up weird number games in my head.

For instance, if a number was on the wall I'd instantly tell myself how much I needed to add to reach a hundred. My love for numbers ran deep. So deep that it wasn't until I was in high school, tutoring middle school kids in math, that I realized my brain worked differently when it came to numbers. Give me numbers and I can divide, multiply, add, subtract, or provide the square root for them in the matter of a second. I thought that was a gift that everyone had once they reached a certain level in learning, but I quickly learned that wasn't the case.

After four years at Clark Atlanta University on a full ride scholarship, I obtained my bachelors in accounting and Maleek gifted me the money to startup my company. We were three years in business, five stars on Yelp, and I was definitely one to toot my own horn so I could confidently affirm that we were the best accountants in town. Of course our competition liked to say that Maleek's status as a successful restaurateur in the city helped bolster my client list rapidly when we opened our doors, but it was the expertise of my team that kept those clients in place.

We were in the middle of January, and Birmingham was experiencing a freezing winter, with temperatures dropping as low as fourteen degrees. That wasn't an issue for me though, I loved the low temperatures. It was nice to finally pull out the cute jackets, scarves, and boots. On days like today, I thoroughly enjoyed living in Mountain Brook. My four bedroom, three bathroom, two story home was a short drive to the Birmingham Botanical Gardens. After my spat with Maleek then the brief encounter between me and Jax, I needed the tranquil setting to help ease my mind. I already made up my mind that would be my first stop after delegating tasks to my employees for the day.

MALEEK PIERCE

Jax caught me completely off guard in the kitchen this morning. His presence was unexpected, we were supposed to meet at the spot before I went downtown to help with the opening procedures at one of my brunch spots. I loved Jax like a brother and didn't want him to perceive me in a negative light, that would be bad for business and my heart.

The fact that the lil nigga pulled off without me, made it clear that he wasn't feeling the shit he saw and I needed to think of a way to smooth it over. It wasn't unusual for Jax to pull up unannounced but he never used his spare key to let himself in. Everyone thought that Kenneth's murder was the catalyst for Jax's change in demeanor and it played a role, but it was really the fact that I brought him into the game and he caught his first body shortly afterwards. He was young, alone, and impressionable; the perfect candidate to replace his brother. I could trust Jax and mold him into the savage I needed by my side while I went legit and got out the streets.

Since I didn't fuck with the rest of my family outside of the few cousins I employed, Jax and Koda were the closest things I had to relatives now, and losing either one of them wasn't an option. I met Koda just a few weeks before I stepped up and took Jax in. After my partner

Kenneth, Jax's older brother, was murdered right in front of us, I trained him up to be the savage he is today. To be real, I don't know who these niggas feared more, me or Jax, either way it goes, I wasn't worried about it because that nigga had my back right or wrong. Growing up, I always wanted a lil brother and the universe blessed me with one when I took in Jax.

I loved that boy probably more than I loved my bitch and never wanted him to see me in a negative light. Fuck it though, the damage was done, and I had until the end of this meeting to think of some fly shit to explain my actions. Easing into the first empty parking spot outside of the warehouse, I scanned the sea of cars and nodded my head once I spotted Jax's truck. Lil nigga might be salty with a nigga but he was still prepared to run this meeting.

Upon entering the warehouse, Jax was the first person I spotted. He stood in his rightful position, in front of all the workers with his arms clasped in front of him all militant and shit just like I trained him. The chatter ceased once my presence was noticed and I was happy they knew I wasn't here to fuck around. Swaggering to the front of the warehouse, I claimed my position next to Jax and didn't miss the fact that he avoided eye contact, this nigga wasn't feeling me right now for real.

Shaking those thoughts off, I pulled the jacket of my Armani suit off and tossed it onto the empty rolling chair behind me. I had legit business to attend to and Koda's slow ass already had a nigga running late for the emergency meeting I summoned the crew here for.

"I'mma keep this shit real brief. You nigga's joined the team knowing that we run a tight ship," I projected my voice over the room, motioning my hand between me and Jax. Silent head nods filled the room just as I expected. "Blane, where the fuck you at?"

Movement ensued among the forty to fifty men in the room and shortly afterwards Blane appeared in the front of the crowd. The nigga was probably older than me but still moved like he was in his twenties. Mouth full of ghetto ass permanent gold teeth and a head full of unkempt dreads, he clearly never had plans to get up out the trap.

"I hear that you had some grievances so today is the day to lay them on the floor. We are a team and if you have an issue let's lay it out on the floor like grown men. Blane you're up first and any nigga after you that had something to say in private over the last few days better speak up because y'all know how I don't like liars."

"It wasn't nothing too crazy," Blane threw his calloused hands up in the air. "I just mentioned that we ain't gone have nobody to help move shit in and out like that after you shot Corey in both hands for mislabeling the money. He is out of commission and we down one person in the stash house during the middle of the month."

I accepted everything Blane was spitting; this lil nigga been down since I moved to Birmingham and took over. However, that didn't mean shit because the ungrateful motha fucka ran his mouth too much, questioning my authority in front of others. Which started a ripple effect, putting me on edge. I had secret listening devices in all of my spots to make sure that a motha fucka wasn't trying to cross me. The snakes slithering beside you will bite you quicker than the ones on the outside. Blane had me feeling like he was trying to start a revolt. Once he got to talking, that lead to other niggas venting, mentioning my name in rooms that they thought I wasn't in.

"Anybody else? Speak up," I urged.

Terry stepped forward, big nigga was sweating like a hoe in church ready to testify. "I uhhh... nothing too major. I just mentioned that we needed to find other ways to handle the niggas that make mistakes. Especially when they ain't thieving, snitching, or fucking off on company time."

I nodded my head, accepting Terry's feedback as well because I already heard that nigga say that as well on the listening device.

POW! POW!

I whipped my gun from my waist and shot Terry and Blane at point blank range. "Anybody else got some shit they wanna say? Speak now or hold that shit until you in the grave!"

The room remained silent, and Jax took charge, signaling with a wave of his hands for the team to disperse while summoning the clean-up crew. Stepping over their corpses, I shook my head at the stupid motha fuckas. For a brief moment, I thought about letting these niggas slide but then the events of the morning replayed in my head. If these fuck niggas wasn't talking shit, I wouldn't have been in a rush to get out of the house this morning. My attitude would've been more relaxed and Jax wouldn't have witnessed me spazzing on Koda. I glanced over at Jax and he still hadn't acknowledged me. After our intense staredown, I wasn't sure how I should approach the lil nigga. I did my best to keep the shit under wraps because domestic violence was a touchy subject for Jax.

My phone vibrated in my pocket as I sauntered into my office. I pulled it out and this bug ass bitch was calling me for the second time today. After adding her to the block list, I slid the phone back into my pocket as a few of my younger cousins approached me.

"Cuz, we wanna chop it up with you in private for a moment," Darnel, the leader of the clique, announced.

I snapped my fingers to grab Jax's attention and his eyes darted in my direction. He pulled his gun off his waist and approached. "Wassup?"

"Ion know, I think some of our crew had something to say so I wanted to make sure my right hand was privy to the conversation."

All five of them scratched their heads and tried to take off like they didn't want shit. "Naw, y'all had some questions or concerns right?" The sound of my voice ceased their movement.

"Naw, we will catch you later," Darnel assured me.

I waved my hands, dismissing their weak asses. The fact that they were blood didn't move me, the only motha fucka I claimed as kin was Jax. He was the closest thing to me, Jax moved like I moved, and never bitched up like these niggas did at the sight of the next nigga holding a gun. Once they were out of sight, Jax placed the gun on his waist and proceeded in the opposite direction without a word to me.

"Jax," I called out to him and he paused, glaring over his shoulder in my direction.

"I gotta go downtown to help open up Koda's Soul Food because the general manager has the flu. When I'm done there I'll need you to take a ride with me."

He silently nodded his head and stalked off. That wasn't like Jax, he wasn't usually quiet. I honestly didn't need Jax to take a ride with me. That statement was more of a temperature check and his non-verbal response told me this nigga was really bothered by my actions so my explanation better be perfect before I regurgitated it. I hated that for the first time since I trained Jax up I had no idea what was swirling around in his brain. Jax usually spoke his mind and never bit his tongue, making it easy to read him. Halfway out of the warehouse I realized I left my jacket and turned to go back in but Jax was already running it out to me.

"Good looking," I commented, ecstatic with his gesture.

It showed that he wasn't too mad, I could smooth this shit out. The last thing I needed was Jax turning his back on me right now. Hopping in my Range Rover, I sped off ready to handle my legitimate business for the next few hours knowing that Jax would have the street shit on lock.

KODA

"Does anyone have any questions about the changes I am implementing going into this income tax season?" I questioned, scanning the faces watching via Zoom. Observing a few head shakes, I took that as a collective no and offered a bright smile. "Great. I hope that you guys are ready to make this money to start the new year. I will also have a bonus for the CPA who brings in the most new clients this season."

"Okay that's what I'm talking about," Will, one of my senior CPA's, piped up.

"Boy hush, you barely converted any new clients last year," Michelle chimed in.

"Alright, I have to go but I love the energy and I pray that y'all keep it up," I chuckled, at their antics. I promise Michelle and Will needed to have sex and get it over with because they bantered like a pair of sex deprived teenagers.

"You right Koda, Ion have to talk," Michelle quipped and Will waved her off.

"Good bye. I will see you guys Monday morning," I laughed. "Make sure y'all direct all questions and concerns to Will for the day. Will only call or text me if it's an emergency."

"Gotcha boss," Will saluted before exiting the meeting.

I followed suit and closed my laptop then stripped out of my professional attire and threw on a Nike jogger set with my running shoes and a hoodie to keep me warm. Grabbing a bottle of water from the refrigerator on my way out of the door, I prayed that my parents weren't busy today, I needed them more than ever right now. The two mile drive to the Birmingham Botanical Garden was nerve racking, I was about to do some shit that I knew would set Maleek off if he found out but I needed it for my own mental sanity. If Maleek did find out, I would just have to make my run for it before I was prepared.

I thought back to the good times, the first five or six years of our relationship were amazing. He never put his hands on me, helped me with whatever I needed financially throughout college and high school then helped me open my accounting firm. If I could blame anything on the change between me and Maleek, I would have to say it was our close proximity. Prior to my high school graduation I lived with my parents, then when I went to college I lived on campus for two years then got an apartment with Simone. It wasn't until I graduated from college and moved in with Maleek that he showed his true colors.

Throwing my car in park, I placed my gloves over my hands and stepped out, happy to soak up some natural vitamin D from the January sun. It was cold as hell but being in the midst of nature was always relaxing for me and I needed it right now. Once I was deep in the garden, I pulled my phone out to call my parents. It'd been a year since we had the altercation that led to Maleek forcing me to change my phone number and cut them off. Unbeknownst to Maleek I conversed with my parents three months ago when I heard my dad was injured on the job and could no longer work. The tear filled reunion was therapy for the soul. I used some bonus money I received from a celebrity client to purchase my parents a home wherever they wanted for an early retirement. Initially, my father declined the offer because he didn't want Maleek to find out and make things harder for me but I insisted and assured him that we would set it up in a trust that wouldn't easily be traced back to either of us.

The call connected and my mother's face appeared on the screen. Jealousy consumed me because my parents chose to retire in Clearwater, Florida and they were sitting out on their pool deck in their bathing suits while I was bundled up fighting the frigid weather that exposed my breath every time I exhaled.

"Koda baby," my mother grinned, a tear already rolling down her cheek.

Guilt consumed me worse than the last time I spoke with them because I could see the hurt written on their faces. My father sat up in his lounging chair and pulled the dark glasses off his eyes so he could get a good look at me through the screen on mom's phone.

"How you doing baby girl?" My father took the phone.

"Good," I instantly lied. "I just wanted to see you guys this morning. I'm taking a walk and it's so cold here while y'all out by the pool living your best early retired lives."

"It would be better if you were here. You're always welcome to join us temporarily or permanently," my mother stuck her head back in the camera.

"I know," I offered a smile.

"Where are you? It looks cold out today, you sure you don't want to come down for a lil vacation?" My dad teased.

"I'm sure, seeing you guys on Facetime today is enough. My company has a lot going on right now anyways. You know people are gearing up for tax season so we are about to be extremely busy with an influx of clients that only come around during tax time."

"No matter what, we are so proud of you," my mom bubbled.

"Always proud," my father added.

"Thank you. Did you guys get the Christmas gifts I dropped in your bank accounts?"

"Yes and I'm glad you mentioned that because it's still sitting, waiting for us to send it back to you but we didn't know how. You've done enough for us. Your mom has a part-time job and my disability check keeps us afloat."

"Mom, why do you have a part time job?" I rolled my eyes at them.

"I can still work," my mom shrugged, taking a sip from her mimosa and that warmed my heart. They were relaxing in the middle of the day, drinking mimosas like they deserved to. "Being home with your father all day watching Sports Center isn't for me. Hell, if your dad's leg wasn't messed up he would still be on the job too."

"You god damn right," he grumbled. "Your mom is just working at a spa as a part time masseuse."

"For now," she sassed. "Those ladies make bank off of facials and things of that nature, I am considering going to school to become an esthetician too."

My dad made the talking motion with his hand behind her head and I involuntarily giggled. "What's funny? You don't think I can do it?" My mom frowned her face up in the camera.

"No ma, I know you can. It can't be any harder than when you went to school for massage therapy but dad is the one doing this," I snickered, making the hand gesture and she spun around to face him. The guilty expression on my dad's face was priceless. He was a big goofball, wrapping my mom up in a hug from behind and the phone dropped down, ending the call. Before I could call my parents back an incoming call from Simone interrupted me.

"Hey boo, I'm going to call you right back," I explained, prepared to hit that red button again.

"No! It's important," Simone shouted into the phone, halting my finger.

"Wassup boo?"

"It's about to go dooooown! The judge I work under just signed off on a sealed indictment with search warrants to hit Maleek's warehouse, y'all house and all of his restaurants simultaneously. I can't say for certain when it's going to happen but it will be within the next seventy-two hours. I'm positive that they are about to get hit with a RICO charge."

"Oh my God," I gasped, sprinting to my car as my heart felt like it was about to jump out of my chest. On the average day my nerves were all over the place due to Maleek's treacherous streak, but the shit was on a new level today. My words were jumbled, my breathing was erratic, and I felt tears cascading down my cheeks for a plethora of reasons.

"You there Koda?" I couldn't respond to Simone because nothing came out. Luckily, my best friend knew me better than anyone else on this earth. My parents tried to pull me away from Maleek but Simone minded her business, and was always the listening ear I needed and that's how our friendship survived. Simone helped me dry my tears and heal my wounds everytime Maleek got out of line. She privately encouraged me to leave and promised not to judge me if I stayed with him, hence why the next words that fell out of her mouth didn't surprise me. "If you want to finally get away from Maleek, now is the time. He's about to go to prison and you can finally be free. I can hear you breathing so I know that you're still there. Please take this out, Koda. You're sharing your location with me so I can see that you aren't in the office and that means something probably happened and Maleek did some foul shit so you didn't feel like going into work on the second Friday of the month when you have your team meeting."

Simone's words didn't fall on deaf ears, I clung onto them, craving additional words for motivation. I know to some this may seem silly, but the fear of staying and taking another slap to the face was a better option than having Maleek come find me. The first time Maleek put his hands on me, I threatened to leave and he responded. *"Don't matter because I'm just going to come find yo ass and bring you back home."* The conviction in his words, mixed with the money and resources that I knew he had access to were always the best deterrent. Maleek meant exactly what he said and had the means to follow through.

"I'm going home to pack my things now. Friday is his long day and he won't be home until late," I uttered.

"Do you need me to come help you friend?"

"No, I'm going to be in and out since you said they also have a search warrant for the house correct?"

"Yeah and they can execute these search warrants at any time so I'd be in and out to be on the safe side," Simone urged.

"Thank you so much Simone," I dried my tears as I brought the engine to life. The car was freezing, and it probably needed a moment to warm up, but I had things to do. "I love you."

"I love you too Koda, call me as soon as you gather your things and leave the house."

"Okay," I assured her before disconnecting the call and pulling out of my parking spot.

Mashing on the gas, I swerved out of the parking spot and floored it to my home. The news from Simone coupled with the impromptu conversation I had with my parents felt like a much needed sign. It was now or never if I wanted to take the leap of faith for a fresh start. To some I was about to tuck my tail and run home to my parents, but I didn't care, my parents were exactly what I needed.

When I made it home I rushed upstairs and pulled my Louis Vuitton suitcases down from the top of the closet and tossed in random items. I didn't care what I brought with me and what was left behind for the Feds to tear apart during their raid because I had money to replace anything I needed when I got where I was going. Gathering the folder with my important documents from the file cabinet, a picture of me and Maleek tumbled out. We were so young and happy in that picture. I was eighteen, moving into my dorm room and Maleek stood behind me like a proud boyfriend. I don't know where that man went because the monster I laid next to at night was no longer him. I placed the picture back into the file cabinet and suddenly the lights flickered then turned off.

My heart thumped rapidly in my chest and I consciously coached myself to breathe. Initially, my mind went to the police and my dumb ass would be swept up in the raid. Then the howling winds slammed the backdoor shut and that thought left my mind. Spinning around to face the left side of the closet, I frantically keyed in the passcode to the safe where my gun was hidden. The three beeps when the safe unlocked made me close my eyes because whoever was in the house would find me with ease now. I clicked the safety off as I heard footsteps entering the room. If it was an intruder, I wouldn't give them the time to get me first and if it was Maleek, he'd be catching a bullet today because I was done with his abusive ass.

I couldn't do this shit anymore. The absence of my parents weighed heavily on me; their faces served as constant reminders of the precious moments I had missed. More than anything, I craved peace, a return to my true self. Ever since I relocated to Birmingham, I had transformed into the woman Maleek desired, losing sight of who I truly was. Our spat last night highlighted how dismal our situation had become, and Maleek clearly didn't have it in him to change. The burden of being the flawless accessory on Maleek's arm, contributing to his impeccable public image became unbearable, especially considering the monster he exposed behind closed doors.

Tears flowed freely because the thought of what would happen next was daunting. I never shot anyone before but I would to preserve my own life. Footsteps entered the bedroom and I held my breath because the silence in the house made everything seem louder. The blackout curtains in the bedroom left it dark in the room and closet but I saw a male silhouette enter the bedroom. They were maneuvering too effortlessly in the darkness for it to be anyone other than Maleek.

With my arms outstretched, I closed my eyes and let off a single shot. Moments later I felt the gun snatched from my grasp and the tears flowed freely. I raised my hand in surrender, prepared for a bullet to the head, slap to the face, or whatever was to come next. Death had to be easy because the suffering that I was enduring with Maleek couldn't be my indefinite reality.

JAX

With Corey out of commission and Blane gone I had to step up and help with the count. As I ran the bills through the money counter, Blane's sentiments resounded within me. While Maleek was off playing businessman, I was left to pick up the slack due to his actions. I don't know if I was agitated after receiving little to no sleep or if witnessing Maleek put his hands on Koda left a bad taste in my mouth.

I was raised to love and protect women, not abuse them. In my eyes, men who felt the urge to put their hands on women were the lowest types of niggas. At the same time, Maleek was my brother, blood couldn't make us thicker. When my back was against the wall and I didn't have anyone else in my corner Maleek always came through for me. If it wasn't for him, I could've spent my teenage years in the foster care system, bouncing from group home to group home.

The irony of it all is I only needed Maleek in my corner because my father was one of those weak ass men who felt the need to put his hands on women. My mother endured that bullshit for years until my dad took it too far, delivering a punch so forceful that she tumbled onto the glass dining room table. It shattered into a million pieces and a shard of glass nicked one of her major arteries. She bled out right in front of us while the weak ass nigga ran off. While I relived the flashback of that day, it wasn't my father and mother but instead Maleek and Koda in their places.

My stomach churned at that shit and my soul was left on fire. After banding the money that ran through the counter, I placed it in the duffle bag and went to wash my hands so I could roll a blunt. Maleek was the reason we were behind schedule and I wasn't about to bust my ass to get us caught up. When I plopped down on the sofa and pulled out my sac of weed I shook my head at the tension in the room.

Usually niggas were smoking and playing music while counting but it was quiet as fuck in here today. I'm positive that my presence was the reason for that. Outsiders feared me but the men within our organization knew that I was the one who put in work and laid niggas down. It definitely wasn't Maleek and his business suits. Today was the first time Maleek had to lift a hand to bust a gun since I claimed my position by his side at the young age of sixteen. Scanning the room, I could sense the tension, Maleek's rash decisions regarding the team were bad for business. We could treat the niggas in the streets like they weren't shit but the men on our team needed to trust us if we wanted them to remain loyal in the clutch.

The silence in the room was needed though, it allowed me a moment to think and clear my mind. This was the first time in years that I was questioning Maleek's leadership abilities and I couldn't remain silent about the shit. Lighting the blunt, I took a long pull while thinking about how to approach the situation. Everything about today felt wrong. From witnessing Maleek put his hands on Koda, to Blane taking his last breath in front of the entire team over some bullshit.

My phone vibrated in my pocket and I pulled it out to see that it was Maleek calling. Taking another pull from the blunt, I debated on whether or not I wanted to answer the phone. Clicking the red button, I ignored his call just for the nigga to hit me right back. I put my phone on DND and leaned back on the couch to finish the blunt, if the nigga wanted to talk he knew where to find me.

After finishing my blunt, it took another two hours to complete the task at hand. With the duffle bags filled with money grasped in my hand, I was prepared to leave the stash but there was a loud knock at the door. Snatching my nine from the table I tossed the duffle bag I was holding to the couch. The entire room was on high alert because everybody knew there was no in or out when we were handling money.

"Relax y'all, it's Maleek." Tyrone, the guard in the back who was watching the security cameras called out to us.

I placed my gun on my hip and reclaimed the duffle bag from the couch but I didn't relax. Maleek was here to try to chop it up with a nigga but I wasn't sure how I would handle him. He knew how I felt about niggas putting their hands on women, and now that I would have to face him solo, I had to admit to myself that I was looking at the nigga funny.

Two of our men went to open the steel door, and as I tried to exit to avoid Maleek, he did an about-face and trailed me back out of the door.

"I'mma slide with you so we can chop it up," he informed me, reaching for one of the duffle bags.

"Bet."

I released my grip on the bag and we sauntered over to my truck. Tossing the bags into the backseat, I rounded the car and slid into the driver's seat to remove the AK from the passenger seat. Once it was safely laying across the backseat Maleek climbed in and we took off.

"Look, I know shit looked bad this morning and I ain't making excuses. I fucked up and lost my temper with all this shit I got going on. We got niggas entrenching our territory, I had to wear a mask in front of all them uppity niggas last night, and niggas on our own side stepping out of line."

"So you hit her? Beat them niggas that fuck up your money, or them white folks that stay playing in your face, if you need to take your frustrations out on somebody. Not Koda, the woman you claimed to love," I vexed, never taking my eyes off the road.

"Jax, I know that shit is a sore spot for you..."

"Exactly why I would've probably respected you more if you kept shit a buck. You been putting your hands on Koda, don't sit up here and try to make it sound like a one time thing. She wasn't phased or super shocked by your actions, she was... was... she was used to that shit," I vented, as the reality settled in for myself as well. Glancing in Maleek's direction, he remained silent, jaws tight as he stared ahead, lost in his own guilt.

"Shit nigga, I'm sorry," he hesitantly muttered as if he were struggling to formulate a response.

"Did you tell Koda sorry?" I inquired as I stopped at a red light. My eyes were locked on Maleek, anticipating his answer so I could assess sincerity.

"No," he answered honestly.

"You need help man," I added, following the flow of traffic. "And you need to leave Koda the fuck alone. Figure your own shit out before you end up hurting her."

Maleek's phone sounded off and whatever text message popped up on his phone had his attention.

"What the fuck?!" He groused, looking from the phone to the road and pointing at the BP gas station. "Pull over here, I gotta make a phone call real quick," he requested.

I hit my blinker and pulled into the parking lot. Once I was in a parking spot Maleek exited the truck and I watched as he took the call, pacing back and forth. He was engrossed in the brief conversation before getting back in the truck.

"Jax, we gone have to speak on this shit later. I can't make the stops with you today. Take me back to the warehouse."

"You straight?" I questioned, noticing that he was all jittery and shit now. His middle and index finger rapidly tapped his thigh, which was uncharacteristic for him. Maleek usually stayed cool no matter what went down, and he took pride in being the one who could keep his composure even when shit got ugly.

"Yeah, just gotta handle some shit quick so push this motha fucka," he directed.

Nodding, I pulled out of the parking spot, ready to get this nigga the fuck up out my face before shit got ugly. If the nigga wanted to be a pussy and lie, I wasn't going to press him. I needed a clear mind to get this money up out of the truck safely. Ion know why he would choose now to try to discuss this shit anyways.

My anger kept me quiet, and Maleek seemed disturbed by that call, leaving the awkward silence between us almost deafening for the duration of the drive. When we pulled up to the warehouse, Maleek damn near jumped out of the truck before I threw the bitch in park.

"We'll finish that conversation later," he announced before closing the passenger door.

I placed the truck in reverse and backed out of the parking spot as he jogged into the warehouse. Leaving that conversation unfinished didn't sit right with me. Driving out of the parking lot, thoughts of my own mother plagued my mind. We never thought that day would be her last day but you never knew with shit like that. Unable to shake the feeling, I cut the wheel to the left and made a u-turn in the parking lot. We were going to finish this conversation today.

Reclaiming the parking spot, I turned off the engine, retrieved my gun from under the seat, and placed it on my hip before stepping out of the car. "Where Maleek went?" I questioned Charles, one of the men guarding the door.

"He rushed into his office."

I jogged to the left of the warehouse, planning to make this shit quick with all of that money in the truck. However, the faint sound of Maleek uttering my name through the cracked door caught my attention and halted my stride.

"Look, I'm gathering my shit now to go into hiding but I'm willing to put all of this shit on Jax if you can work a deal for me. What the fuck you think I keep him with me at all times for? He makes the majority of the big moves, shit if I can feign ignorance depending on the type of evidence they got that'll work for me too. If I can escape this with my reputation intact I'll have a bonus for you." Maleek detailed, stuffing documents into a duffle bag.

Seething in anger, I burst through the door, and Maleek's wide eyes met mine. The betrayal cut deeper than I could have ever imagined. Every blunt we smoked talking shit, every laugh we shared while sipping D'Usse was now tainted by the foul taste of deception. The air hung heavy with the weight of our irrecoverably shattered bond. I experienced a surge of conflicting emotions—betrayal, hurt, and a deep sadness that seemed to echo through the core of my soul. This was my nigga, more like my brother; Maleek raised me up in this game from a pup. Clearly that shit was one sided, it didn't mean a fucking thing to this snake ass nigga.

Maleek made a move, and as the shock wore off, my killer instincts kicked in. Rushing across the room, I hopped over Maleek's L-shaped executive desk, sending his unfinished bottle of water and papers fluttering everywhere. He unleashed the beast in me, and I caught his hand before he could pull the gun from his desk drawer. With a swift left hook, I connected with Maleek's jaw, causing blood to gush from the deceitful bastard's mouth. His eyes momentarily rolled to the back of his head and I didn't let up. My right hand clenched Maleek's shirt as I pummeled his face.

The echoes of my harsh breathing and my fist colliding with his face resonated in the confined space.

"You tryin' to fuckin' play me, bitch ass nigga?! Me, your brother?" I questioned, releasing the grip on Maleek to stand up.

I was prepared to stomp this nigga out but the water that fell on the floor caught me offguard and I slipped. Grabbing a hold of the desk to break my fall gave Maleek and his bloodied face a moment to make a run. Once I was back on my feet I noticed Maleek opened up a hidden door next to his bookshelf. I whipped my gun out and let off a shot as this nigga slipped inside. Emptying the clip out of frustration, I already knew I wouldn't be able to get into that room but I rushed over and searched for a way to open the door.

"What the fuck? You good?" Charles pried as a few other men rushed in behind him.

I paused as other men trickled into the room at the sound of gunshots. "Any of y'all know about this door? Where does it lead to?" I barked, rubbing the barrel of my gun against my temple out of angst.

"Nigga, what door?"

"Maleek just slipped into some type of secret door that was right here. Where the fuck does it lead to?" I quizzed, rubbing my hands around the space where the door previously opened. Lifting my gaze to the screens on the right side of the wall that showcased different angles from the security system. However, Maleek was nowhere in sight though.

"Ain't but one door in this motha fucka," Charles replied.

"Clearly not. Do you see the motha fucka in here?" I roared, freezing the entire room. Niggas knew how ugly shit could get when I was on one.

"Ion know shit about no door but we can look around," Charles offered, raising his hand in surrender as he backed out of the room. Breathing deeply, I scanned the faces of the men who looked to me and Maleek for guidance and debated on what I wanted to say or do next. I didn't have any real information besides the tail end of Maleek's phone call.

"Shit is hot and some big charges coming down and that fuck nigga Maleek was in here talking about snitching on me. Do what the fuck you gotta do based on that information because I'm gone," I explained, brushing past Charles on my way out of the office. The men behind me were in shambles, spouting off questions that I didn't have time to answer, they could believe it or not.

Sprinting towards the door, I confirmed that Maleek's car was still in the parking lot. Rushing over, I shot out all four of his tires. I don't know what that nigga had in mind, but it was clearly every man for himself with that snitch bitch on the loose.

Hopping in my truck, I sped out of the parking lot and my first stop was Maleek's house. My foot didn't ease off the gas until I pulled into their driveway. Leaving the engine running, I hopped out of the truck and went around the house to enter through the back, closer to their circuit breaker. Using my key, I entered the house and went straight to the utility closet and flipped the main circuit breaker. The wind slammed the backdoor closed and I heard three loud beeps sound off from upstairs.

Rushing in that direction, I entered the bedroom looking for Koda. When I turned the corner to enter the closet, my eyes bucked at the sight of Koda aiming a gun at me before a bullet went off. I ducked and the single bullet missed me. Snatching the gun from Koda's hand I scanned her frightened face. For a silent second I thought Koda knew she was shooting at me, but something in my spirits told me she thought it was Maleek.

Her eyes popped open and regret spread through them. "Jax, I thought you were... I'm so sorry..."

"Come on Koda. I gotta leave the city, shit hot and yo nigga about to get hit with some charges. If you trying to get away from that nigga now is the time. I know he be over here putting his hands on you. I only asked earlier because if you said yes, I would've known you were ready to leave that nigga and I was gone go up there and handle that bitch ass nigga. But I know how y'all women can be, you'll forgive the nigga and be mad because I knocked his shit loose."

"No, I have to get out of here," Koda sobbed. "It's real bad too, Simone called and told me that there is a sealed indictment with search warrants to hit Maleek's warehouse, this house, and all of his restaurants simultaneously. This is my only chance to make a run from Maleek and I'm taking it, so please just let me go."

"Good, we on the same page so I don't have to convince you to leave that no good motha fucka. He is about to try to put all this shit on me and work himself a deal. I ain't laying down like that for the laws so I'm about to leave town and you coming with me. I'll get you wherever you want to go, but you gotta get the fuck away from that nigga before he hurts you."

"I know," Koda broke down crying.

Embracing Koda in my arms, I rubbed her back, granting a brief moment for her to release her emotions. However, we had to get the fuck on asap.

"Koda, you gotta get your emotions together so we can slide."

"I'm ready," she assured me, wiping her tears away with the sleeve of her jacket.

"I just need to grab something out of here. You need some cash and I can't waste time going to my condo downtown to get my go bag but I know where Maleek keeps his," I released the grip on her and passed her the gun back.

Snatching her bags from the floor, Koda trailed me into the hallway where I opened up the crawl space and pulled a dusty Louis Vuitton bag out. I unzipped it and confirmed its contents before leading Koda out of the house. My next move had to be my best move.

MALEEK

Gasping for air, I stumbled into the dimly lit panic room and leaned up against the wall.

POW! POW! POW!

The sound of gunshots on the other side of the wall sent me rushing away from my position, desperate to put more distance between me and the mayhem. I knew that the wall was bulletproof but I'd rather be safe than sorry. My heart was pounding in my chest like an HBCU drummer. The echoes of chaos from my office reverberated through the narrow corridor, and the acrid smell of gunpowder lingered in the air, reminding me of how close I almost came to catching a bullet.

My legs felt like jelly, weakened by the adrenaline rush that helped me up off that floor once Jax slipped. Realizing that Jax overheard my conversation with the lawyer shook me to my core for multiple reasons. Was Jax always my fall plan? Absolutely. However, that doesn't negate the fact that I loved my young nigga. He was like a brother to me, been by my side making shit happen and laying motha fuckas down since I brought him into my world and I hated that it came to this. Unfortunately, self preservation would trump any bond I had with anyone.

Now that I had a moment to recuperate from the ass whooping Jax blessed me with, my survival instincts kicked in. Stepping deeper into the panic room, I flipped a switch to turn on the lights and grabbed the AR-15 I had sitting on a pallet of water. I pressed my back against the cold, rough wall, taking long ragged breaths as I tried to collect my thoughts and formulate a plan. The taste of fear lingered on my tongue, as the tunnel provided safety from Jax, but I had to get the fuck out of here ASAP. Ain't no telling when the Feds planned to execute those search warrants and I couldn't be trapped in here when they did. This panic room was some new shit I was slowly working on after one of my business partners mentioned having one.

My face was throbbing and I gently tapped my lip, realizing it was leaking. Rushing into the bathroom, my face was fucking unrecognizable. Breathing deeply, I almost wanted to rush out of this room and blow Jax's head off. I wasn't scared of him but the nigga had about six inches on me, and I've watched him kill a few motha fuckas with his bare hands. If I had to go toe to toe with Jax I couldn't fuck around. Plus, I ain't have my shit on me because I was coming back from the restaurant or else I would've blew that nigga noodles out.

I knew how to choose my battles wisely though, if I exited the panic room now, he would have the upper hand because I wouldn't be able to see beyond the doors. Pulling a rag from the rack above the toilet, I took a moment to clean the blood from my face. Excruciating pain accompanied every tap to my face, forcing me to move at snail's speed.

I didn't know how much time had passed while I cleaned my face and rinsed the blood out of my mouth but it was silent in the office when I exited the bathroom. My phone was lost in the scuffle and there wasn't a clock in sight. Leaning the AR up against the side of the pallet of waters, I tore it open and pulled one out. With shaky hands, I twisted the cap off and guzzled half the bottle. Moving closer to the door, I listened intently for any sound of movement. My head was pounding and I felt myself getting weaker by the second. The bright lights were irritating the fuck out of me and I hit the switch to cut them off. Realizing that something was wrong with me. I decided to gamble the shit. Gripping the AR, I slowly opened the door with the barrel of the gun leading the way.

The office was empty and a slight sense of relief shot through me as I closed the door and locked it. Scanning the room, I found my phone on the floor beneath my desk. Collecting the phone, I glanced up at the cameras and noticed the warehouse was completely empty. When my eyes landed on the money room, the view of empty tables that were previously stacked high with money that was collected from the streets, I felt my chest cave in. Rushing out of the office, I moved my aching body into the money room and dropped down to my knees after receiving visual confirmation.

"WHAT THE FUCKKKKKKKK!" I roared, while disabling the security cameras from my phone.

I planned to use that money to get low and now it was gone. Taking a deep breath, I had to get my shit together quick. Scrolling to Koda's number, I initiated the call and it went straight to voicemail. Dialing the number again, I received the same results and that infuriated me more. That bitch wasn't doing anything too important at that fucking office. Pulling my keys out of my pocket, I remote started my Porsche and rushed out of the door just to find my shit sitting on four flats.

Panic settled in, the situation became more dire by the second. Koda's office wasn't too far from here and I placed another call to her front office.

"Thank you for calling Stellar Financial Services, this is Michelle, how may I help you today?" She bubbled into the phone.

I couldn't stand this loud mouth bitch, I would've preferred anybody answer the call other than her. Me and Koda got into it in the office one night when we thought we were there alone, just for this bitch to be in her office working late. She stuck her nose in our business, told Koda she deserved better, and it took everything in me not to knock the spit out of her mouth for speaking on me. Since that day she didn't fuck with me and the feeling was mutual. Last time I called up there, Michelle answered, and the dumb hoe hung up on me when she was supposed to be transferring my call to Koda. Then she must've taken the phone off the hook because when I called back the bitch wasn't ringing through. Little did she know, Koda paid for that shit as soon as she got home. It was Koda's responsibility to keep her phone charged at all times just in case I needed her, and she failed me that day.

"Michelle, I know you like to play games but I'm on all that today. Transfer me to Koda's office and don't be with the bullshit or I swear to God I'll come up there and beat yo ass."

"I keep my baby Glock on me nigga so I wish you would fucking try it," she spat before disconnecting the call.

Closing my eyes, I winced because forming my angry scowl left me in excruciating pain. Taking a seat inside of my Porsche, I allowed my aching body to relax. I placed another call to Koda and received the same results, so I had no choice but to bite the bullet and call her office again.

"Look mother fucker, Koda didn't even come in today. Probably because of some shit you did, so stop calling up here. Call your house phone instead of tying up our line. Koda is out and so is our receptionist so I'm working and manning the phones. I don't have time for a pissing contest with your weak ass today," she ranted and hung up before I could get a word in.

If Koda wasn't in the office and she was at home I could get a message to her through our home's security system. Clicking around my phone until I found the security app, I felt a sense of panic because the internal security cameras didn't have signal, and I could only see the exterior of the home. After staring for a moment, I saw Koda rushing out of the house. Pressing the microphone button to give me access to speak over the camera, I called out to her.

"Koda, I need you to come pick me up from the warehouse! It's an emergency!"

The last syllable rolled off my lips as Jax exited the house with the emergency Louis Vuitton duffle bag that I kept in a crawl space clasped tightly in hand. My veins ran cold as I observed the full picture. Jax had my shit and Koda was dragging a suitcase out of the house.

"Eat a dick, bitch ass nigga!" Jax exclaimed, pointing his middle finger at the camera. Koda stood frozen at the sound of my voice because I brought fear to her heart, I knew it, I could see it in her eyes. She was ready to go against whatever the fuck Jax talked her into doing.

"Koda, Ion know what he told you but you better remember who the fuck I am and the things I'm capable of," I vexed.

"You better remember the same shit about me before you open yo dick suckas and mention me to the Feds," Jax snarled, dropping the duffle bag. He pulled a nine from his waist and shot the camera down, leaving the *no signal* message on that camera as well.

JAX

All of the crying Koda did left her ass exhausted and she was knocked out an hour into the drive. Four hours later, and her ass was still asleep when I parked the truck in a dimly lit alley on the south side of Valdosta.

Gorgeous, captivating, breathtaking and all that shit could be used to describe Koda. Now that all bets were off, I allowed myself to do something I hadn't done in years, I admired her gorgeous face. Since the first day I spotted Koda in the early morning, waiting for the bus on my first day of middle school, I had a crush on her pretty ass. Her light blemish free skin, juicy ass natural pouty lips and bright eyes helped form my first real crush. I know it might sound like I was lusting after my brother's girl, but I didn't bat an eye at her until I saw Maleek put his hands on her.

I always had a soft spot for Koda and Simone. We came up together, lived in the same neighborhood, went to the same middle and high school. If I'm being honest, I met Koda first. I told Maleek and my late big brother I had a crush on her, and they told me to step to her. I never followed their suggestions or anything like that because we had a friendship and I was afraid to ruin that, but the puppy love feelings were there and Maleek was well aware of them.

Koda ran with the nerdy girls though and they weren't fucking with a young nigga like me. Not because I wasn't handsome or no shit like that, but because she was two years older than me. When I was a sophomore, she was a senior and they loved those older niggas that already had cars and shit. Even with all of that said, when I learned about Maleek's relationship with Koda, it was big ups to my brother for snagging one of the most beautiful women I ever saw in my life. Anger and grief wouldn't allow me to give a fuck about that shit. Now looking back, the shit seemed sinister, like maybe the nigga went after her on purpose.

Not only was he too old to be dealing with Koda back then, he had all the bad bitches his age fawning over him. He had money, power and respect, and with that came hoes. Yet he was entertaining Koda. I was probably the only person who knew that they were messing around before she turned eighteen because Maleek was my guardian, and I lived with the nigga when I wasn't out of town handling business.

"You two looking for a good time?" A woman dressed in a red cropped fur and a mini dress in this cold ass weather approached the truck with a seductive smile on her face. The bitch had to be freezing, it was seven o'clock and the temperature was in the 30s. Her wild eyes told me she was high as fuck and probably wasn't feeling shit.

"Get the fuck on," I grumbled. Frowning my face up, I waved her off and that woke Koda up.

"Where the fuck are we?" Koda queried, observing our surroundings.

Fear immediately washed across her face and I spoke up to quell her apprehension. "One of my cousins is about to drop a whip off for us to switch into and I'mma leave this truck over here so somebody can steal it."

"Why?"

"If Maleek or the police are looking for it they'll be off our actual trail for a minute. I don't plan to see the inside of a prison cell and I've been planning an escape route that even Maleek didn't know about for a few years. Funny thing is, I didn't keep these plans away from Maleek because I thought the nigga would snake me. I just never wanted anybody knowing about my cousin, he a tax paying citizen and shit, didn't want him in the mix." I replied. "So where you trying to go tomorrow?"

"To my parents house."

"Fuck no. It'll take Maleek and the people he work with no time to find them," I argued.

"That's something that I also thought about before I bought my parents house. Maleek doesn't know about it. I paid for it with my own money and it's not in their names. I'm good at moving money and assets, remember? Please just trust me on this, the home is owned by a revocable trust that I made sure wouldn't trace back to me. My parents don't even live around here anymore, they live in Clearwater, Florida, a small city that he would never think to come to."

"You sure, Koda? Ion wanna leave you there just to have that nigga hunt you down," I finally turned to face her.

"I'm positive, Jax. I wouldn't play with my own life like that. Above all else, my parents are too old to be mixed up in the bullshit I have going on," she assured me.

The mention of Koda's parents was what persuaded me. I hadn't seen Koda's parents in years, but I knew she loved them in spite of their estranged relationship. Now my mind had me wondering, was Maleek's abuse the catalyst for the distance in Koda's relationship with her parents? I wanted to ask her but my mind instantly switched gears when two cars pulled up behind us.

"Alright Koda, I'm trusting what you're saying," I conceded, watching the cars in my rearview mirror.

Marco flashed his lights in the Honda Accord twice and the car behind him followed suit, flashing their lights three times. With the signal confirmed, I gripped my AK and stepped out of the car.

"Come on, that's my cousin and his wife," I informed Koda.

She reached for the handle and exited the car as well. I grabbed the three duffle bags and Koda grabbed her suitcase and trailed behind me.

"Jax, what have you gotten yourself into?" Tracy, Marco's wife, questioned as she exited his car dressed in a nightgown and bonnet. "Got my husband pulling me out of the bed in the middle of the night and driving way over here."

"I always told y'all I would let y'all know when I was making my exit. All y'all need to know is I'm doing that," I kept shit brief.

"Who is this you got with you?" Marco inquired, eyeing Koda.

"Nobody," I replied sternly. "And if by any chance anybody ever comes asking questions, you didn't see me with anybody either."

"We got you," Marco nodded, passing me the keys to the ride. "Do you need anything else besides the whip?"

"Nah, I'm straight. When I make it to Cuba I'll check in," I assured Marco.

"Alright, take care of him for me. He might be ruthless, but every savage has a heart," Marco addressed Koda and she nodded in understanding.

I didn't have time to dispel his suggestion that we were romantically involved. My only concern was getting the fuck from around here, drop Koda off, then flee the country without any bullshit. When I formed my getaway plan, Koda was never a part of that so this trip to Clearwater already had me off course. It would add a few additional hours onto my trip to Key West where one of my other homies who owned a boat would take me to Cuba.

I was aware that there was a high chance that shit could go left in my line of work, forcing me to disappear, but I didn't anticipate it happening so soon. The last thing I saw coming was Maleek betraying me. I always thought I'd slip up, kill a nigga that caught me wrong at the right time, and have the murder boys looking for me. Or getting caught slipping with the re-up, but naw, my own brother snitched on me. The pain cut deep, and didn't shit usually bother me. Trauma was a constant in my life, I was always waiting for the other shoe to drop. I never thought Maleek would be the one to put a knife in my back, twist it, and leave me bleeding out in the cold.

"I doubt Jax needs anybody to take care of him. He's the one who has been taking care of me these last few hours," Koda expressed, staring up at me with bright eyes.

Done with the mushy shit, I snatched the keys from Marco and trekked towards the car. "Come on Koda."

I heard her feet moving behind me in the darkness. Throwing the duffle bags into the backseat, I turned to gather the things Koda brought with her before jumping into the Honda and hitting the road again. About an hour away from our destination my eyes got too heavy to continue driving, so we stopped and got a room for the night. I couldn't wait to get this shit over with.

KODA

Waking up in the hotel room this morning, I experienced a sense of safety and freedom. Leaving Maleek had always been a source of dread, but this marked the most liberating experience I'd had in a long time. Slipping my feet into my slippers, I approached the double sinks and stared at my reflection in the mirror. This was my new beginning, it was a long time coming and I was going to take advantage of every opportunity that was presented to me. No more stuffy business events that made me feel like we were still in the Jim Crow era. Those days of concealing the tattoos I got in college, at Maleek's insistence, were behind me. This new chapter in my life is all about Koda and embracing the things that bring me joy.

With little hygiene products, I sucked it up and utilized the hotel hygiene amenities before getting dressed. I still didn't have a phone, but Jax did some shit putting a new chip into one of his phones twice since we hit the road. My first order of business was grabbing a phone once I got settled in.

A sudden knock at the door startled me until I heard Jax's voice. "Koda, you in there?"

Exhaling, I relaxed and rushed towards the door. The weather here was much warmer than in Birmingham, and the sun greeted me before

Jax's face entered my peripheral. The bright orange lighting around Jax intensified as I stared up at him, casting a warm glow on his features. Even the mug on his face couldn't take away the rush of optimism I received. The sunshine seemed to carry a promise of brighter days ahead and I was loving it.

"Come on Koda, I'm on a tight schedule," Jax explained, tapping the Rolex on his wrist. I accepted the bag from Dunkin Donuts and Jax shook his outstretched hand for me to grab the iced coffee too.

"Okay, I'm ready, I can eat this in the car."

"Alright, I'll grab your luggage," Jax offered as I scanned the contents of the Dunkin bag. Pausing at the sight of the sourdough breakfast sandwich and hash browns, I looked back over at him.

"You remembered my order from when we were in high school?"

"We had that routine every day for a year. I remember Simone's order too," he responded, grabbing my suitcase from next to my bed. "I remember you like them sudoku puzzles too, so I grabbed one out of the gas station too."

Staring Jax down, I almost forgot how much time we used to spend together. His older brother Kenneth used to drop us off at school, and we'd stop at Dunkin Donuts every morning so he could buy us breakfast. If we needed rides home after practice, Kenneth always looked out for me and Simone. After Kenneth was murdered and Jax disappeared, our relationship perished. When Jax resurfaced, I barely saw him unless it was in passing, and even then, he'd offer us a head nod and keep it pushing. I never took Jax's distance personal; I didn't even have a sibling, so I could only imagine what it was like to lose one. Then, when I moved in with Maleek after graduating from high school, we saw each other more often, and the friendship slowly re-emerged. If there was ever a time that I needed Maleek and he wasn't available, Jax would be right there.

There was even a time or two that I snuck and went to the club with Jax and Simone while Maleek was away on business. Of course he had no idea I was sneaking out, he just thought I was accompanying Simone because she was always out with them, living the life as a young twenty year old should. Meanwhile my ass was sitting up in the house with curling rods in my head before ten o'clock on most nights.

Trailing Jax out of the hotel room, I paused when I saw the housekeeper pushing her cart down the hallway. She was about my size and I decided to be a blessing. Starting fresh would start with a new wardrobe so I could wear whatever the fuck I wanted and not whatever Maleek decided would work for him.

"Excuse me, I have a bunch of new and gently worn clothes that you can have if you'd like," I offered, taking the suitcase from Jax. Initially her face said *bitch I don't need your charity* until she noticed the Louis Vuitton pattern on the luggage. The suitcase alone was valuable and I was willing to give it all up.

"Sure," she bubbled, accepting the suitcase. "Thank you so much."

"You're welcome. I hope your year is off to an amazing start," I chirped before we re-entered Jax's room where he collected the three duffle bags and we were on our way.

A little over an hour after we left the hotel the GPS said we were one minute away from our destination. Turning onto the unfamiliar street, a wave of emotions washed over me as I laid eyes on the house I had only viewed in photographs on the internet. In person, the house was impressive, and the additions my parents made to the landscaping were breathtaking.

The thought of seeing my parents' faces in the flesh after years of distance shot my anxiety through the roof. "You straight? You breathing hard as shit," Jax inquired, turning the radio down.

"I'm fine," I lied, internally coaching myself to slow my breathing down.

"Your parents are going to welcome you with open arms, no matter what happened, trust me. My grandparents always let my mom come home. It was always her who ran back to that nigga, crushing their hearts every time. Don't do that shit to them, don't do that shit to yourself," Jax grumbled.

Growing up in the same neighborhood as Jax, I knew all about his family history and felt bad for triggering him with my own bullshit. His jaw was tight and his eyes now reflected a distant sadness. I could sense the weight of my actions lingering in the air, and the silence between us became a heavy reminder of why it was imperative that I stood on business.

Jax parked in the driveway and we wasted no time exiting the car. I rounded the car and quickly embraced Jax in a firm hug. "You don't have to worry about me, Jax. I promise I'm not going back."

"You better not, Koda," Jax expressed before breaking the hug and cupping my chin, forcing me to face him. "You deserve so much more and you're fucking perfect, if a nigga don't value you, he doesn't deserve you."

"I know," I sniffled, and he gently wiped away my tears.

Out of embarrassment, I diverted my eyes in another direction until he mumbled my name. "Koda."

Nervously glancing toward Jax, I braced myself for potential judgment and doubt. As our eyes met, I noticed a shift in his energy, there was adoration and concern staring back at me. The gentle, kind side of Jax that I hadn't seen in years was staring back at me. It brought on a feeling of nostalgia, before life got real for us. His protective nature and genuine concern revealed a depth to him that went beyond the tough exterior.

In that moment, I felt a newfound appreciation for the man standing before me. He made me feel safe. It wasn't the distance between me and Maleek, the fact that his abusive ass had no idea where I was or how to find me that made me feel safe, it was Jax. My childhood friend would never allow anything to happen to me. I sensed it in the kitchen yesterday morning but now it was confirmed. His presence was suddenly a security blanket that I would have a hard time letting go.

"Koda, baby!" I heard my mother shriek behind me.

Tearing my gaze away from Jax's, I followed the direction of the voice. My parents' smiling faces forced the floodgates to open, and tears cascaded down my cheeks as I rushed to meet them in the middle of their perfectly manicured lawn. My parents smothered me in their embrace, the feeling of their love was a stark contrast to the pain I'd endured for so long. Their tears mingled with mine, as we expelled the hurt from the past.

In that moment, the weight of my struggles lifted, replaced by the unconditional parental love they had for me. We stood together as a family, ready to rebuild the bonds that time and distance had strained.

My mother was the first to break the embrace as she pulled her body back to get a good look at me.

"You're here in the flesh please tell me this means you finally decided to leave that man and come home, Koda," she blubbered, her eyes searching mine for the confirmation she desperately hoped to find.

"Yes mom, I was hoping that I could stay here until I got on my feet. My exit was inevitable, I just needed to find the strength but that's why I had you guys retire here after dad's leg injury so I could have a safe haven to come home to."

My mom sobbed and pulled me in for another hug. "You know we always wanted you to come home. The guest bedroom is set up and our house will always be your home."

"Absolutely baby girl," my dad added in, kissing both of my cheeks.

"Jax?" My mom questioned, finally noticing my security blanket.

"In the flesh," he greeted her. She rushed over and dramatically hugged him too and he shook hands with my father.

"Ohhhhh this was meant to be, isn't it Karl?" My mom snuggled up next to my dad, staring me and Jax down.

"Yeah it is."

"What do you mean by that?" I queried.

"I'm almost done with dinner and after talking to you yesterday I decided to whip up some of your favorites."

"You making a crab boil?" I bubbled.

"Well your second favorites," my dad chimed in. "Smoked mullet, and seafood rice."

"I haven't had smoked mullet and seafood rice in so long that it should be at the top of my food hierarchy now," I chirped.

"Now that I got you with your family I'm going to head out," Jax addressed me.

"Absolutely not. You're going to sit at our kitchen table and enjoy this food before you leave. I said it was meant to be because I made enough seafood rice to feed all of us and Karl smoked more than enough mullet. Come on and get washed up," my mom took his hand, leaving Jax no room to refuse.

The moment we crossed the threshold, I felt like I was at home.

My mother's signature lavender scented candles filled the living room, offering an inviting atmosphere, just like when I was a child. The tears started again and I felt Jax's strong hands rubbing my shoulder. Clearwater was going to be my home, I was going to have a fresh start, and Jax my security blanket couldn't leave me yet.

JAX

Watching Koda reunite with her parents sent a bunch of emotions I hadn't experienced in years rushing back to me. When my brother died, the shit turned me cold. I felt like the world was against me, God had forsaken me, and I had no idea why. From the time I could remember, my life was filled with trauma, watching my dad abuse my mom was some shit that no child should've had to witness. Luckily as me and Kenneth got older, the abuse lessened because he was just as big as my dad. It took for Kenneth to knock our dad's head into the wall one time for him to realize he couldn't handle his own son. I got to view first hand how a nigga could monkey stomp a woman but couldn't handle a real man.

After our mom died, Kenneth got in the streets, stepped up to the plate and took care of me to the best of his ability. My grandparents were both struggling with their own ailments and in nursing homes so they couldn't take me in. Kenneth and Maleek were guiding me through life until Kenneth was taken away from me, and that just left Maleek.

When I disappeared after Kenneth's murder, it was because me and Maleek were in his hometown of Birmingham, putting in the work and laying the foundation for us to take over the city when his uncle retired. I caught my first body when I was sixteen, a few months after Kenneth's murder. Maleek had me making drops and a nigga thought shit was sweet so I put my murder game down. I wasn't naive though, and Maleek was honest, he had me putting in work because of my age. If I was caught there would be less consequences due to my age. I wasn't even mad though, the shit made me feel powerful and I knew from that day forward I'd rather be the hunter over the prey any day. From that day forward that's what I became, there was no room for anybody to feel like they could fuck with me. Not even Maleek, the nigga who brought me into the drug world.

I was proud of Koda though, she was packing up to leave that nigga before I pulled up. There was no convincing at all, I could tell that she was done by the look in her eyes. I'd seen that shit in my mother's eyes too on our many trips back to my grandparents house when she said she was done with my pops. I just pray that Koda would stay strong like my mother wasn't able to. Learning that Koda was already putting shit in place to disappear, gave me hope for her.

"So Jax, we haven't seen you in as long as we've seen Koda. What type of work are you doing these days?"

"I'm in logistics," I confirmed, taking a sip from the glass of water.

"That's nice," Mrs. Allen nodded her head. "Oh, how is Simone?" She questioned both me and Koda.

"Simone is okay, still working as a law clerk in Birmingham," Koda replied.

"I never thought Simone would turn into a snitch, shocked the hell out of me," Mr. Allen blurted out with a shrug, causing me to laugh.

"She's not a snitch daddy," Koda giggled. "She's a law clerk."

"Same damn difference, she work for them boys in blue, locking niggas up," he shot back.

"Is she ever planning to move out of that position and follow her dream of becoming a lawyer? I never understood why she chose to become a law clerk when she had firms offering her top dollar. Hell, work her way up to be a judge at least, instead of being his assistant with a fancy title."

"I don't know ma, it's not something I drill her about."

"Well you should. You started your own financial firm, encourage

Simone to do the same. Speaking of your firm. How is that going to work with you being here?"

"I haven't quite thought that far ahead ma," Koda confessed, finishing her last bit of food. My eyes landed on hers because there was no way she would be able to have anything to do with her business if she wanted to remain free of Maleek. Yet, another topic I'd have to discuss with her before I took off.

"Jax, are you going to be sticking around for a little while as well?" Karl questioned me.

"Nah, I got some business to tend to."

"I hope that business doesn't have anything to do with Maleek," he shot me a knowing glance.

"Nah," I kept shit short. If Koda decided to run down the story of how we ended up here to her family, that was her decision. As for me, I wasn't explaining shit to anybody.

"Well, I'm about to clear the table and roll a blunt," Karl announced, standing to his feet.

"I'mma help you with that," I jumped to my feet, prepared to lend a hand.

It had been more than twenty-four hours since I last smoked, and a nigga was feening for a blunt. My ass was rushing to make it to Key West so I could grab some green. I didn't have people down here, and I should've added trees to my exit plan because a nigga needed some.

Thirty minutes later, the table was clean. Mr. Allen started the dishwasher, and Koda's mom took her to Target to grab a few things. Trailing Mr. Allen into their backyard while rolling a blunt, I had to admit that this shit was nice. The short walk to one of the empty seats near a small table that held a lighter and ashtray had me rethinking life. I loved living in my downtown apartment because of the amenities. I'd gladly trade in the onsite dry cleaning, full-service bar, and twenty-four hour fitness center for my own pool in a silent backyard to fill my lungs with marijuana smoke.

Igniting the blunt, I took a long, deep pull, instantly gratified as my craving was satisfied. Exhaling the weed smoke, I eyed the blunt and nodded my head. "I needed a blunt bad as fuck so I was willing to take anything, I thought it was gone be some reggie, but this shit gas,

Mr. Allen," I grinned before taking another pull and passing him the blunt.

"I have a medical marijuana card due to my injury so I've been blessed to legally obtain some of the best from this dude named Banks. It's a black owned dispensary too. Ion fuck with edibles, I took one once and thought the lord parted the sky to come grab my old ass. If you like 'em, take 'em," he offered.

"Ion fuck with them either. I like to get high but a nigga need to function, gotta be able to protect myself at all times."

"I feel ya," he conquered.

"So you finally got Koda to leave Maleek? I fought tooth and nail to get my baby girl away from his no good ass."

Mr. Allen's question caught me off guard but it didn't surprise me. "That's something you gotta take up with your daughter. Hol' up, I gotta take this call," I announced, checking my ringing phone. It was my homie with the boat, the second to last piece of my exit plan, and I couldn't miss this confirmation call.

"Yoooo," I answered the phone, walking around the house until I reached the front lawn.

"Aye my man, I just got your text and I have some bad news."

"Come on Alvaro, don't do this shit to me," I groaned, knowing he was about to hit me with some bad news. "When I gave you that fucking money to buy the boat, I only had one request. Get me the fuck out of the country if the need arised."

"My apologies, Jax, but you hit me at the worst time. My daughter wanted to take a little trip for her sixteenth birthday and we are out at sea now. I'm not bearing all bad news though because we were already on our way back home. It'll take me a few days to get my family home and then I'm on my way to Key West. Can you lay low for a few days?"

"What choice I got? Just hit me with an ETA once you get your family home safely."

"I got you," he stated, and ended the call.

Taking a deep breath, this shit had my nerves bad and I needed to hit that blunt again asap. Being stuck in Florida waiting to see if Maleek would really snitch wasn't the way I planned to spend the next few days. I planned to be in Cuba where the shit wouldn't even fucking matter. Biting the bullet, I dialed Simone's number next and her ass didn't pick up. My last resort was checking the Birmingham jail search and sure enough, there was Maleek's mugshot with a trail of charges listed. There were so many that I didn't give a fuck to read them all. I would've preferred if this nigga was free, that would've meant my name would be out the mix. Either way, I believed every word he spit, that nigga was probably enjoying a two piece and a biscuit while telling all of my motha fuckin' business. Maleek was the last nigga I needed turning on me, he knew where the bodies were buried, and the revelation of my darkest secrets would put me under the jail.

Mrs. Allen's Nissan Versa whipped into the driveway and I could see her and Koda smiling through the windshield. This was where Koda needed to be.

"You okay Jax?" Mrs. Allen quizzed as she exited the car, catching my attention.

"Yeah, we had a long drive and the food was good, I'm just tired," I explained, rushing over to grab the bags for them.

"Well we have a guest bedroom, go in there and take a nap," she encouraged, as they trailed me up the driveway.

"Just show me where it is and I'mma definitely lay it down," I confirmed. My head was spinning and with all of the shit I had on my mind, I needed a nap to regroup before I figured out where the fuck I was going to wait for Alvaro.

I sat the bags down on the dining room table, and Koda showed me where the guest bedroom was and I knocked out as soon as I met the plush mattress.

The sound of movement in the room forced my eyes open. It was pitch black in the room but her silhouette in the darkness was evident, allowing me to relax. I was a light sleeper, always ready for whatever, but I wasn't prepared for what happened next. Koda slid into the bed next to me and snuggled up against my left side like a puzzle piece finding its place, or like a cub seeking refuge with its lioness. Since the day I discovered that Maleek and Koda were a thing, I let my crush go, plus I knew I had too much hate in my heart at that time to treat anyone right. Hence, why I stayed the fuck away from people in general during that time. Koda became my nigga's girl, almost like a sister in law and unlike that nigga Maleek, I respected the code. Now that his mask was off and I was questioning whether or not the nigga ever had genuine love for me, that sense of loyalty I had for the nigga was null and void.

I knew I offered Koda a sense of security, the way she looked up at me when we were standing in her parents driveway told me so. That nigga Maleek probably hadn't brought her a sense of safety in awhile, he was too busy offering up abuse and misuse. I stared up at the ceiling with both hands behind my head and allowed Koda to get comfortable. Suddenly, I felt her soft hands remove my hand from behind my head and reposition my arm around her back. Following Koda's lead, I pulled her in closer and rubbed her back in a soothing manner, not wanting to seem like a creep ass nigga, but I also didn't want her to feel rejected. I almost felt guilty, but this shit felt amazing. Her soft body pushed into mine had both of my heads spinning.

"I don't want you to go, you make me feel safe," Koda whispered, just as I was about to start overthinking shit.

Receiving clear, audible confirmation that I made Koda feel safe touched a deep chord within a nigga. If I'm being honest, it had been a long time since anyone looked at me for a sense of security. I was usually seen as the grim reaper, or the nigga you didn't want to catch on a bad day. Shaking my head, I brought myself out of fantasy land and acknowledged the reality of the situation.

"I can't be stuck under your family's roof and shit."

"Well where are you planning to go?"

"Cuba, my buddy has a boat that'll get me there in a few days. Stop thinking about me, worry about yourself."

"Well, you can stay here for those few days, we can explore the city together. I know you didn't get to experience life as an average teenager after Kenneth was murdered, but it's never too late."

"Nah, it's definitely too late, this ain't no fairy tale Koda. If that nigga is going to snitch I gotta be far the fuck away from here."

"Fine," she huffed, sitting up in bed.

Koda was clearly trying to relive her adolescent years because she was acting like a spoiled brat who didn't get her way. Slapping the button to turn on the lamp sitting on the nightstand, she spun around to face me, her arms folded across her chest. She was wearing a tank top with no bra on, and her hardened nipples were staring up at me while her hair was in a messy bun.

Yeah, she was definitely taking it back to almost a decade ago. When she'd walk out of the house in a pair of sweatpants and an oversized t-shirt to run errands. Since she moved to Birmingham after graduating college you wouldn't catch Koda out in a relaxed fit like this. She was always dressed like a rich nigga's wife. No matter what time you popped up at Koda's house, you wouldn't catch her in a bonnet or a tank top. I always thought that college changed Koda, morphed her into a prissy bitch that wore heels around the clock, and kept her face beat at all times.

"Since you can't, can you leave one of your guns with me?" Laughing hysterically, I sat up in bed to meet Koda's gaze since she looked like she wanted to shoot a nigga now.

"What the fuck you know about a gun, Koda?"

"I know I need protection, and you made me leave Maleek's gun in Birmingham," she looked away from me.

"I thought you said Maleek wouldn't be able to trace the house back to you."

"He won't, I just want to be on the safe side," Koda clarified. "If you don't want to leave one of your guns, I understand but can you take me to buy a gun before you leave?"

"Fuck no."

Koda gasped, squinting her eyes at me. "Fuck you, Jax."

Reaching for my gun on the side of the bed, I brought it into view and Koda's eyes instantly widened. Gripping her wrist, I pulled her hand towards me and placed the deadly piece of steel in her delicate palm.

"Hold that motha fucka," I ordered, relinquishing my hold on the gun. "If you have it you gotta learn to use it and be prepared to squeeze that trigger if you pull it on a nigga like Maleek. You can't be scared, you can't hesitate, you gotta be ready to blow his fucking head off. Give that nigga the one way ticket to hell that he deserves. Above all else, you gotta be done with the nigga to do any of that."

"I'm really done, Jax and I promise I will learn to use it."

"Alright, Koda. I have to chill out for a few days before my homie can meet me in Key West. I'll stay here and I will take you to the range a few times and if you prove yourself, I'll get you the gun before I leave."

"Okay," Koda nodded, her hand stiff in the same position I left the gun in.

Shaking my head, I retrieved my gun and placed it back on the side of the bed. I barely got any sleep last night, but my body was ready to make up for it now. Mr. and Mrs. Allen's home was so inviting. It was like we were in sync, by the time my head collided with the pillow, Koda turned the light off and snuggled back up on my side. Except this time, I placed my arm around her on my own, she felt good in my embrace and I was soaking up the feeling.

KODA

Waking up to the melodic sounds of New Edition emanating from the speakers signaled my location and the day of the week. Every Sunday my mom woke up early to clean the house with the music blasting before making breakfast. It was good to see that after eight years, things hadn't changed. The jovial feeling swiftly dissipated as I noticed Jax was no longer beside me in bed. My mind instantly went to the worst case scenario, Jax leaving without saying goodbye. The mere thought made my heart ache and at that moment, I was able to acknowledge that it was more than safety, Jax had my head gone. If you met him, he would have your ass gone too.

Jax was super light skinned and the first thing you would take note of was the perfect set of pink pussy eating lips he was blessed with. The full jet black beard covering his face created the perfect contrast with his light skin. Last night after Jax fell asleep, I fantasized about running my hands through his beard once he willingly placed his arm around my back. Although Jax was Maleek's friend, a bitch wasn't blind. I always noticed his handsome face attached to a beautiful body that was covered in intricate tattoos. I was just dumb enough to respect my relationship and never cross the line. The memory of suspecting Jax had a crush on me in high school suddenly became vivid, and now, the tables had turned as I found myself attracted to him.

The way he cupped my face in the kitchen after witnessing Maleek put his hands on me had my heart fluttering then. I just couldn't acknowledge it and I definitely couldn't admit it. Then Jax came back to the house for me, knowing he needed to get away from Birmingham to save his own ass, he still thought about me. It was his selflessness for me.

Sitting up in bed, I snatched the covers off to confirm my suspicions when the door flung open. The natural lighting from the large windows in the house gave Jax that warm glow again. Now that I mentally acknowledged my feelings, I'm sure it was written all over my face because of Jax's response.

"Why you look like *yo* nigga left you for dead or something?" He laughed, stepping into the bedroom with the three duffle bags.

"I thought *he* did," I admitted, shrugging my shoulders. Sliding off the bed, I slipped my feet into my bedroom shoes.

"Man, stop that," Jax shook his head, tossing the duffle bags onto the accent chair near the window before approaching me. He slowly placed his hands on my waist and I felt the tips of his fingers sink into my flesh.

My breathing hitched as I stared into his dark eyes. They told the story of his rough childhood and deadly demeanor, and I think that's what drew me in more. Getting this up close and personal view allowed me the opportunity to admire his features. From afar he was fine but being this close, Jax was definitely one of the most handsome men I ever encountered.

Then Jax smiled, exposing his perfect white teeth. It wasn't a regular smile either, Jax's smile told me he would fuck the shit out of me and I bit my bottom lip, hoping to let him know that I would let him. I don't know if it was the forced proximity or the level of security Jax made me feel, but I was ready to douse the fire that was burning inside of me since I climbed into the bed with him last night. While laying in bed, I thought about Maleek, not because I wanted him back or missed him. However, I was questioning whether or not Jax would ever look at me in that light due to his close friendship with Maleek. I could've been fucking Jax while I was still living under Maleek's roof, and that still wouldn't have compared to the bullshit he put me through.

"Koda, I know you don't plan to sleep all day!" My mom's voice brought me back to reality and like a pair of sneaky ass teens, we jumped away from each other.

"I'm up, coming to see what you got in the fridge so I can make everybody breakfast," I replied, exiting the bedroom.

When I entered the kitchen, my mother was already pulling items out of the refrigerator. My heart felt so full, I missed my parents and I was going to cherish every moment I lived under their roof again.

"Relax by the pool with Mr. Allen, we got breakfast," Jax announced, entering the kitchen.

"Trust me, I won't argue," my mom quipped, placing the pack of bacon down on the counter.

She scurried out of the kitchen while Jax washed his hands. I opened the cabinets one by one until I located the pots and pans.

"I didn't think you knew how to cook," I quipped, sliding past Jax to rinse the skillet in the sink.

"I'm grown as fuck, why wouldn't I know how to cook?"

"I don't know, you just don't seem like the type," I admitted, looking up at him while I sat the skillet on the stove.

"I gotta *eat* don't I?" He questioned before wiping his tongue across his bottom lip.

The manner in which Jax emphasized *eat* and the extension of his tongue sent my body into a tizzy. Had me thinking about exactly what I would love for Jax and his enticing pink lips to do to me.

"So what do you want to eat with bacon and eggs? French toast or pancakes?" I quickly changed the subject, turning the stove on high.

"It's your world, whatever you want Koda," Jax commented.

Everything he said felt like it had a double meaning today and if he didn't cut it out, nobody would have breakfast. We maneuvered throughout the kitchen preparing the food like an old married couple that spent years cooking together. I made the pancakes and he prepared the bacon and grits. While I whipped up the eggs, Jax went outside to smoke with my dad, and my mom came in to help clean and cut strawberries. As soon as we were alone, she didn't waste any time questioning me in private.

"Alright, when you initially arrived with Jax, I thought maybe he wanted to make sure you made it home safely. But then y'all slept in the same guest bedroom when there are two separate guest bedrooms, so spill it. How did you go from Maleek to Jax? I'm not here to judge, as long as he doesn't control, manipulate, or put his hands on you, I wouldn't have given a damn if you decided to date Maleek's father." My mom rambled.

"It's not like that, ma, I promise. I told you some stuff went down and we both had to leave Alabama. Jax fell out with Maleek and I decided that I was finally ready to leave him."

"Soooooo that means you had to sleep in the bed with him? He had to hold your waist and stare into your eyes like his long lost lover this morning?"

"You saw that?" I gasped, covering my face.

"You don't have to be embarrassed, Koda," she encouraged. My mom gently took my hands away from my face and cradled both sides of my cheeks in her palms. I smiled because she saw right through me and it was reminiscent of conversations that we had about Maleek in the past. This time, my mother's eyes held a glimmer of hope and affection, in stark contrast to the usual pain and distress that conversations about Maleek brought to her gaze. "We just want to see you happy Koda, that's it."

"I'm finding my way back to happiness, but I didn't come here because I'm dating Jax now. I came here because this is where I want to be, my relationship with Maleek is over and Jax just makes me feel safe. Sure we have done some subtle flirting since leaving Birmingham but it's still a little weird."

"It's not strange; neither you nor Jax ever had any business around Maleek's overgrown manipulative ass at such young vulnerable ages," my mom huffed, frowning her face up. She vigorously shook her head, dispelling the negativity that mentioning Maleek brought up. A smile adorned her face as she planted kisses on my cheeks. "Like you said, find your way back to happiness and take your time along the way."

"I am," I confirmed with a smile. If I fell into some lust along the way, then that was okay too.

"What is that cheesy grin about?" My mom inquired.

"Nothing," I snickered.

"What y'all in here laughing about? I hope the food is ready because we hungry," my dad stated, entering the kitchen to wash his hands with Jax behind him.

"The food is ready, help carry something to the table after you wash your hands," my mom instructed.

We enjoyed breakfast like a big happy family. The smiles that filled the room were contagious and my heart felt full. My dad and Jax cracked jokes with their high asses, and it felt like all was right in the world.

MALEEK

eep!

Beep!

Beep!

My eyes struggled to open because they felt heavy as hell. The room was a blurry haze, and slow beeping caught my attention as some of the most excruciating pain I'd ever experienced hit me immediately afterwards. Every part of my body ached and my head was pounding profusely. Allowing my eyes to focus on my surroundings, I realized I was in a hospital room. Perplexed, I tried to piece together the fragments of memory that were missing, but my efforts only intensified the pain.

The memory of my lawyer's phone call surged to the forefront of my mind, prompting me to jolt up in bed. Battling through the pain, I was ready to get the fuck up out of here. Lifting my right arm, I felt resistance and looked down to see that I was cuffed to the bed. My heart rate increased and the door swung open as three officers rushed inside, flickering on the lights. Blinking rapidly beneath the harsh lighting, my memory offered a quick refresher on how I ended up here.

Looking down at the phone after Michelle hung up on my ass, I paced the concrete, debating on who would be the best person to call. After watching them disloyal nigga's on my team run off with my money, I damn sure couldn't trust them. The last person I could count on was Simone. After receiving her answering machine, I shot her a text.

Me: Call me. 911. I need you to pick me up from the warehouse.

While waiting for Simone to respond, I started walking away from the warehouse. I had to get far away from this warehouse and the drugs to help my case. Before I could get out of the massive parking lot, a row of black trucks with police lights bent the corner. Making a swift about-face, I took them boys on a chase. They had to put in work if they wanted to put cuffs on my black ass today. I spent time in the gym daily and ran for sport, so it was a track meet out here.

Even in my hard bottoms, I was out running their out of shape asses. Focusing on what was in front of me, I never looked behind, but I knew they weren't close enough to catch a nigga. That was until we ran into the back fence. Dressed in the suit and hard bottoms, I mentally prepared myself for the obstacle ahead of me. Willing myself to move faster, I braced myself to scale the fence. Jabbing my right foot into the square I used my arms to hoist myself up. Halfway up the fence, I felt a sharp pain and my body started convulsing violently, these motha fuckas tased me. My body stiffened and I plopped to the ground like a ton of bricks. I held my hands out, ready to surrender but these dirty motha fuckas had other plans.

"You making us run nigger?!" I heard one of the officers yell before all hell broke loose.

Tactical boots, fists, and collapsible batons were putting a beating on my ass from all directions. Initially, I was shocked, but after a stomp to the face, dizziness set in. Instinctively, I curled up in a ball to protect my head and neck, praying this shit worked because I never got jumped before. The ass whooping seemed to last forever and then everything went black and I woke up here, feeling like I got hit by a Mack truck.

"Maleek Pierce, you have the right to remain silent..." This smug motha fucka started reading my miranda rights before I could speak to the doctor about how much damage these dirty crackas did on me.

By the time he was finished, a doctor barged into the rooms. "We should've been in the room first when Mr. Pierce woke up to assess his health. This can wait a few minutes," he commanded.

The officers shot him a few death glares before one looked at me.

"We're going to be right outside so don't try anything stupid, like fleeing again."

My icy glare met his and I offered nothing but the cold stare until they were out of the room.

"Glad you're awake, you had us scared for a little. I'm Dr. Crawford and you have been out since Friday evening when the police brought you in and we completed CT and MRI scans of the head, ultrasounds of the heart, and imaging of the spine. Thankfully, everything looks fine but we are still going to keep you for at least another 48 hours due to your loss of consciousness," he explained before completing a few tasks. Examining my eyes with a light, asking me to follow his finger with my eyes, and a few other simple tasks before offering a thumbs up.

"As the officers informed you, you are under arrest but I already called your lawyer to let him know you are awake, and he should be here any minute now. He has been up here once a day since the police brought you in. Stay strong brotha," he nodded.

"Thank you," I uttered lowly. The doctor turned to leave and the police wasted no time re-entering my room. "Lawyer," I commanded.

"And his lawyer is right here." Chad's chipper ass entered the hospital room right behind the police. "My client has explicitly invoked his right to legal representation, and as such, any attempts at an interview or interrogation are categorically denied. My client, a victim of a severe physical assault resulting in a coma at the hands of BPD, lacks any substantiated evidence supporting his arrest. I have already initiated legal proceedings to have the charges expeditiously dropped, and a hearing is scheduled for the morning. I advise the law enforcement personnel present to maintain vigilance at the door, and furthermore, I strongly recommend refraining from any further interaction with my client. Now I request an uninterrupted moment with my client to discuss the unfolding legal proceedings."

"We'll have officers on the door but if he changes his mind and would like to talk..."

"He won't, but we appreciate the offer," Chad cut him off, giving the officer his back.

That right there is exactly why I keep the blond hair, blue eyed white boy around. He was smart as hell, and your head would spin when he was talking that legal shit. The officers exited the room and Chad went to ensure the door was fully closed before approaching my bed.

"Maleek, you lucked up big time," he celebrated. "When they executed the search warrants they found the warehouse completely empty. No soldiers, no money, no drugs, just walls and security cameras that don't record. There is no way in hell I don't get the judge to drop your charges tomorrow. Plus we will prop you up on the zoom call tomorrow for court and let the judge see your fucked up face..."

"Damn, it's that bad?" I mumbled, sitting up further in the bed.

"Yeah, it looks terrible, but that's going to work in our favor too. I'm going to get the charges dropped and secure a hefty settlement for your pain and suffering. The DA's case was weighing heavily on dope on the table or any evidence that they would have retrieved from the warehouse that they had under surveillance."

"You serious?"

"Absolutely, I just need you to sit tight, let me do all of the talking and we will be in the clear soon."

"Wait, you said there were no drugs in the warehouse?" I questioned, anticipating his response.

"Clean as a whistle," he nodded, rubbing his hands together. "I held a press conference yesterday and fed the reporters the story of a prominent businessman being railroaded by BPD. Your parents even came down to speak on the news. This is definitely going to drum up business for me."

My monitors emitted random beeps, and an abrupt tightness gripped my chest. I checked for my money because it was an immediate need but the thought of them niggas taking the stash never crossed my mind. There were some unscrupulous motha fuckas and it was official, my team was dead, and I didn't know how I would rebuild this shit. Reality was settling in, them niggas didn't fear me, they feared Jax and with him gone it would be an uphill battle to keep my foot on the dope game's neck.

Before I knew it, the doctors rushed back in and ushered my lawyer out. I willed myself to breathe as they shot something in my veins and sleep consumed me again. That was probably for the best because rage was taking over me. Fuck a petty ass lawsuit, fuck these charges. These unloyal motha fuckas ran off with my money and my drugs and I was cooped up in a hospital bed, unable to make a move to get shit right.

KODA

Laying across my parents' guest bedroom, I completed a sudoku puzzle with my bottom lip poked all the way out. My parents left for a day date, and Jax decided he was moving into an Airbnb for the duration of his time in Florida. I was happy that Jax was staying but it hurt my little feelings that he left me. Sitting up in bed, I realized I was being a ridiculous clingy bitch. Yeah we spent the last two days together around the clock, but I knew I was being ridiculous.

Simultaneously, I couldn't control the sway of my emotions, because it was refreshing to feel again. I couldn't quite put my finger on what I was experiencing until I found out Jax left last night; his departure left me with a sense of sadness. It made me realize that I was on autopilot with Maleek and I hadn't felt anything for quite some time.

"Get dressed, I'm about to take you to the shooting range, show you a lil something. See if you really 'bout what you hollin' 'bout," Jax expressed, entering the guest bedroom. I damn near jumped out of my skin because I was just home alone, wallowing with my internal thoughts.

"How did you get in here?" I questioned as he plopped onto the bed next to me dressed in an all black Nike outfit.

Taking a deep breath, I looked away from Jax and plopped back onto the bed to focus on the ceiling because this nigga was so fine. The only thing on my mind was seeing what that dick was hitting for but, I controlled myself and kept to my side of the bed.

"Mr. Allen gave me the spare key before I left this morning."

"He what? He didn't even give me a key yet," I side eyed Jax.

"Shit, maybe they don't trust you like that," Jax laughed. "Now get yo ass up and come on. I'm trying to get over there before this four o'clock traffic hits."

"Alright, I'm ready," I slid out of the bed, and grabbed the slides I bought out of Target on Saturday.

"You wearing that?" Jax pried.

Looking down at the pink joggers and a Muppets graphic t-shirt, I scanned my relaxed fit. "What you trying to say?" I inquired, leaning back and folding my arms across my chest.

"Don't screw yo face up like that, you too pretty for all that shit," he tugged on my arms, pulling me closer to him. "You look beautiful, stop playing."

"I'm saying," I mugged Jax, pulling my arms out of his grasp. "It sounds like you calling me ugly."

"Stop playing, you know you been some fine shit since high school and you know that shit. I asked because I haven't seen you relaxed like this in forever."

"Maleek ran around looking like an astute businessman so I had to look the part, it's what he wanted. Me personally, if we were going to the grocery store or running to Target I'd prefer to be comfortable, fuck being cute. Do you know how uncomfortable stilettos can be every day? When I left college and moved home, Maleek tossed all of my sneakers and replaced them with heels," I shrugged, reminiscing on the bullshit I used to put up with.

"Sweatpants, no make up, lil knock off Yeezy slides, you're still fucking beautiful. Believe that. You can doll that shit up or step out dressed down; either way, you're still going to have niggas looking. But them niggas don't deserve you," he expressed.

The sentimental moment swiftly ended when Jax released the grip on my waist and exited the guest bedroom. I dropped my slides onto the floor, slipping my feet into them before following Jax out of the door. Silence filled the car as I had a million and one items to check off my to-do list.

"What are you thinking about over there?"

"Nothing," I lied because there was a laundry list of shit running through my mind.

I needed to buy a new car, phone, and figure out what I was going to do about my business. That was the one piece of the puzzle I hadn't figured out yet. Stellar Financial Services was my baby, one of my proudest accomplishments, and the only reason why I hadn't left Birmingham. There was no doubt in my mind that my team was holding it down, the accounts were stacked so payroll would go out. However, Maleek was the co-owner and I didn't know how I would run my business without leading him back to me.

After signing waivers, renting a gun, and purchasing target ammo, we put on ear muffs and entered the range looking goofy as hell. As soon as we entered the compact space, the sharp scent of gunpowder filled my nostrils and the popping from the guns shooting caught me off guard.

"Chill, beautiful. You said you want a gun, this what comes with it. Shoot this bitch without the earmuffs on and it's going to be louder." Jax informed me.

"I'm okay," I assured him.

"Alright, first lesson. Keep a firm grip, and never point this bitch at yourself. Comprende?"

"Comprende," I nodded.

"Alright, just watch me, and I'mma show you how you need to be able to shoot if you want me to buy you a gun," Jax explained, as he demonstrated how to load the gun.

When he was done, I stood off to the side and watched him shoot at the target, emptying the clip before placing the gun down. It was sexy as hell to watch him so focused and when he pressed the button on the side to bring the target back, he didn't miss.

"Well, you don't have to be that good, but at least hit a few targets and make sure that you ain't scared. Now load it up, you watched me do it, you got it," Jax instructed.

I was nervous as hell but I slid the bullets into the clip and offered a bright smile when I was done. Jax went over the parts of the gun, how they worked and made me show him I could load and unload the gun before actually showing me how to shoot. After instructing me to pick up the gun, Jax eased up behind me and guided my hands to the proper position. His hard body felt heavenly colliding with mine and I felt a shiver shoot down my spine. I willed myself to focus on the gun because the charged atmosphere made the air crackle with anticipation.

"Now, focus your sights on your target." He requested, gesturing towards the distant silhouette as he stepped to the side. "Take a deep breath, relax your shoulders, and align the sights with your target," Jax instructed and I nodded my head. "Make sure your feet are planted and when you're ready, squeeze the trigger and make sure you don't jerk it." I followed Jax's instructions, sending my first shot echoing through the range. The recoil surprised me but a huge smile spread across my face because I did it and whether I hit the target or not, I was ready to master this too.

"Alright, do it again," Jax urged from a few steps behind me. "Imagine it's time for you to protect yourself and aim for the head, make sure a nigga never get up."

I closed my eyes and took a deep breath, before focusing on the target. Jax's presence gave me confidence and when I squeezed the trigger, it was exhilarating so I did it again and again until the clip was empty. Placing the gun down, I turned to face Jax and he nodded his head before pressing the button to pull the targets back.

"Not bad," he complimented, taking the target down and replacing it with another one.

I felt a sense of accomplishment, as he urged me to continue until we were out of bullets. After leaving the range we stopped in AT&T and I bought a prepaid phone for the time being. Then we grabbed some food at Tropical Smoothie and I opted to sit outside. I was loving every second of the Florida sun.

"We gone fucking bake out here," Jax complained, taking a bite out of his wrap.

"I love it, it's been cold as fuck in Birmingham," I bubbled, taking a sip of my smoothie.

"I prefer cold temperatures, I love being able to throw on my Pooh Shiesty and my coat before leaving the house at night," Jax explained.

"Speaking of leaving the house at night. Where did you go to last night?"

"I told your parents, they didn't tell you this morning? I went to get an Airbnb."

"Oh, is it nice?" I pried, ignoring his question because my parents did tell me but I was salty that he didn't.

"It's straight, nice lil house for the next few days."

"I'd like to see it." I tossed the idea out there instead of openly inviting myself over to his house, his presence was intoxicating and I didn't want to leave him yet.

"Let's make a deal, let me get out this sun and we can head over there now. A nigga hot," he negotiated, balling up the wrapper that his chicken wrap came in.

"Okay," I shrugged, closing up my caesar salad.

Jax tossed his trash and we took off. The Airbnb that Jax secured for his stay was only a few minutes away and it was niceeeee. There was no doubt in my mind that I was staying here with Jax until he left. It was hot as hell after eating outside but I loved soaking up the sun. Jax, on the other hand, was clearly still hot because he tore his shirt off as soon as we entered the house.

I hadn't seen Jax shirtless since high school and the bird chest he used to rock was replaced with a slightly muscular build and countless tattoos.

"I'm about to go take a shower," Jax announced. "Don't break shit in here."

"Boy hush," I sassed.

Floating around the house, I admired the paintings on the wall and was inspired to decorate my living room in royal blue and gold whenever I finally got my own place again. When Jax finally returned, he had a blunt dangling from his lips. He plopped down on the couch, interrupting the rerun of Girlfriends I put on the TV.

"Ain't nobody about to sit here and listen to a bunch of bitches yapping," he interrupted the silence. Standing to his feet, he swiftly yanked me up and gently guided me out of the back sliding door.

"You were just complaining about me taking you to a hot ass outdoor restaurant," I quipped.

"The sun went down, it's about to get nice and cool out here now that the sun went down," he explained.

"Is this what you left me to go do last night? Relax under the stars?" I questioned, plopping down on the wicker patio furniture.

"Nah, I just ain't lived under nobody's roof since I was what? Shit, seventeen. Your parents cool and all but I need to walk around with my dick swinging if I want to," he explained before taking another pull from the blunt.

"And you didn't invite me because you didn't want me to see that side of you?" I inquired, cuddling close to him as he filled the space with weed smoke.

"You ain't ready for all that, Koda."

My heart rate increased and I felt a puddle forming between my legs. I don't know why but my hormones were in overdrive and I had been super horny since we got to Clearwater. Before, I thought it was because I was used to Maleek climbing on top of me nightly, and he went from wanting to have sex three or four times a week to a week drought. I declined sex Thursday night but Maleek was busy in the streets or working prior to that. No matter the cause, my body was craving Jax and that was another feeling I hadn't experienced in a long time. Staring down at Jax, I had yet to respond. I was in my head so bad about the feelings I was experiencing for him.

"What?" Jax questioned, staring back at me.

Instead of responding, I did something I had been dying to do all day. I leaned down and planted a kiss on Jax's lips. It was just a peck and I halfway expected him to push me away but he caught me by surprise, gripping the back of her head and deepening the kiss. His lips felt as heavenly as they looked and there was no turning back now. Beneath Jax's grasp, I flung my left leg over Jax and slipped my body on top of his. I felt his dick grow beneath me and my body went into overdrive.

Grinding into Jax's lap, I pulled away from him, nibbling on his lip in the process. "I'm finna fuck the shit out of you, Koda," he explained, pulling his dick out.

I licked my lips at the sight of his dick with the perfect mushroom head staring up at me. Gripping a hold of it with both hands, I slid down and sucked the head into my mouth. Making sure his dick was coated with my saliva, I went to work. I don't know why, but I felt like I wanted to prove some shit to Jax and have his head gone. After giving a little attention to the head, I jerked his dick in an upward motion while allowing my tongue to trail down his shaft until I got acquainted with his balls.

The size, the girth, the complexion; everything about his dick and balls was perfect.

"Fuck, Koda, go 'head, do your thang," he moaned, running his hand through my hair.

Gliding my tongue back up to his head, I slurped every inch of his dick into my mouth until I felt myself gag. "Nah, don't bitch up Koda, handle this dick," he encouraged. I looked up at Jax while I kept sucking, with his motivating words, I couldn't bitch up. Bobbing my head up and down, he started meeting my rhythm, thrusting into my mouth until I felt the grip tighten on my hair. "I'm about to come and you better swallow all that shit," Jax commanded and ohhhh that turned me on even more. As he requested, I swallowed every drop then offered a meek smile after releasing his dick from my mouth.

"Shit, girl you the fuckin' truth," Jax exhaled. I got up from my squatting position in front of Jax and collapsed on his chest. "The fuck you doing? Come sit on this big motha fucka." He questioned and I noticed his dick was still rock hard.

I was perplexed, Maleek was my only sexual partner and once he came, the night was over. Clearly that was not the case with Jax, and I loved that for me. As much pleasure as I got from giving him head, I knew I would thoroughly enjoy the feel of him inside of me. He gripped his dick and stroked it slowly while waiting for me to follow his command. I must've been moving too slow for Jax because he gripped my hips with his free hand, and pulled me up from the chair with him.

Pulling me into his chest, I felt a trail of kisses down my neck as his hands slipped into my joggers and found their way between my slit. "Damn this pussy wet for a nigga," he rasped into my ear as I threw my head back into his chest.

With every word Jax had me open in more ways than one. I reached up to do something I'd been dying to do for the past two days. Running my hand through his beard with ease, I emitted a low moan because this man was perfect in every way. As the thought ran through my mind, my joggers were snatched down, and Jax bent me over the wicker chair and pulled my thong to the side before thrusting into me. With one hand on my hip, he took control and thrust in and out of me.

"God damn, Koda. This some good ass pussy," Jax grunted as I gripped the chair to give me some leverage.

Throwing my ass back, I felt every inch of Jax deep inside of me and I careened my neck to get a good view of him. At the sight of my face, Jax wrapped his arm around my stomach and turned us around so he was sitting on the chair, and my back was up against his chest.

"Gimme kiss," he demanded, while wrapping his strong hand around my throat. I obliged and leaned up to connect my lips with Jax's and he devoured my lips while thrusting into me from below. Sloshing sounds filled the backyard because I was super wet and I felt that tingling in the pit of my stomach.

Breaking the kiss, I felt Jax release the grip on my neck then guided his hand up my shirt and beneath my bra to fondle my sore nipples. "I'm cumming! Fuck!" I squealed as the orgasm ripped through every inch of my body, leaving me spent. Jax continued his assault, dragging out my orgasm longer than I'd ever felt. When I thought I could collapse into his chest, he pulled his dick out and allowed his nut to fall into the grass.

Kicking my joggers off, I didn't care that I was ass naked outside, I felt carefree as hell and high from the sex. Jax turned me around to face him and our lips connected again. He lifted me off my feet and I wrapped my legs around his waist, sitting my pussy on his stomach as he carried me inside. I was ready for Jax to fuck me in every hole, he had me that open.

JAX

Waking up with Koda's wild hair all over my chest was the best feeling I'd experienced in a long time. Looking down at her naked body all over mine had my dick hard already. She stirred in her sleep, rubbing her hands further across my chest, repositioning her leg so it was on top of mine. Gently pulling her off my chest, Koda turned on her back with her mouth slightly open. I leaned down and planted a kiss on her lips, then trailed down her neck and across her chest.

"Well good morning," she smiled down at me as I kissed her bare stomach. Her back arched beneath me as she stretched.

"Good morning, beautiful," I greeted her before placing a gentle kiss over her perfectly shaved pussy.

My dick felt at home buried deep inside of Koda but I hadn't had the pleasure of tasting her yet. Everything about her was intoxicating and the nectar that leaked from her slit was no different. Lapping up her juices, I forced those beautiful moans from her lips. Her manicured fingers glided across my scalp and I loved that shit. Twirling my tongue around her clit, I enjoyed every intimate moment with her sweetest treasure in my mouth.

"Fuck Jax, right there," she encouraged as I slipped two fingers inside. Her hips bucked beneath me before she tried to squirm away from me. Pulling my fingers out, I gripped her hips to hold her in place as my tongue catered to her clit. "Wait stop!" She screamed as I pulled that nut out of her.

Listening to her moans had me ready to fuck. I licked up her slit before looking up at Koda as she smiled at me. Gripping my dick with my right hand, I used my left hand to pull her down towards me. The contagious smile she wore suddenly disappeared and a look of panic shined through.

"What's..." Before I could finish my question, Kodo shoved me to the side and bolted into the bathroom.

I laid in the bed, dick going limp as guilt consumed me. Koda probably regretted all that fucking we did now that the sex high wore off. In the midst of my guilt trip I heard her throwing up all in the toilet and those thoughts disappeared. She was sick.

"You straight?" I questioned, entering the bathroom.

"No," she choked out after flushing the toilet.

I watched the scowl on her face as she rinsed her mouth and washed her hands.

"You sick from what we did or you just sick?"

"I'm just sick, Jax," she assured me before turning in my direction. "I don't regret anything we did last night. I'm about to get dressed so you can take me home."

"Yeah."

Koda's lips said one thing but her demeanor said otherwise. If she regretted the shit it was too late for that shit. A nigga was hooked on her, this was some unimaginable shit. How many niggas get this close to their older high school crush and they still look good as fuck? Not many at all. The ride to her parents house was silent and Koda pecked my cheek before getting out of the car. I drove off and knew that if shit was meant to be Koda knew how to get in touch with me.

Over the next twenty-six hours, I didn't hear from Koda and that shit was fucking with my soul. I dropped her off at her parents house around ten o'clock and it was noon the next day. Biting the bullet, I tucked my pride and called Koda for the second time since I dropped her off. Her ass didn't answer and I sat there for a moment while I finished the blunt then grabbed my keys to drive to her parents house. I was good and high, the perfect recipe to be on some bullshit. When I pulled up to Koda's house both of her parent's cars were gone and I knocked on the door, praying her ass was here so we could discuss this shit alone.

KNOCK! KNOCK! KNOCK!

I waited for a moment as I heard movement in the house. It had to be Koda, her parents loved a nigga, they wouldn't leave me standing out here.

"Open the fucking door, Koda!" I called out.

As expected the lock turned and the door opened moments later.

"The fuck wrong with you? Before we fucked you acted like you wanted to be in a nigga skin. Now you acting like you can't answer the phone, shoot a nigga a text."

"It's not like that, Jax."

"Well what's it like then, Koda?"

"I was just about to call you back after I took a nap," Koda explained, running her hands over her head.

Shaking my head, I brushed her to the side and entered the house.

"I gotta tell you something and please don't judge me," Koda spoke to my back.

"What?" I spun around to face her. Koda had my nerves fucked up and she probably knew it. I was feeling a little deja vu because the last bitch that started her confession with *don't judge me* came back to tell me she burnt me. After fucking Koda raw this was feeling eerily familiar. The fact that she stood here looking at her nails without spitting that shit out wasn't making shit no better.

"Dawg, you burnt me?"

Koda burst into a hysterical fit of laughter, but I ain't find shit funny. "What? Why would you think that? How many bitches burnt you? You about to stress me out worse because I didn't even make you wear a condom the other night."

"Just one bitch and I learned my lesson, ain't fucked a bitch raw since then and I go get checked every six months so I'm clean as a whistle."

"I don't have anything I just... ummm..." she stuttered, looking down at her feet.

"Man up then Koda, if you finna go back to that nigga just say that. You don't have to coddle me," I grimaced.

"I'm not going back to Maleek, ever!" She proclaimed. "I need you to take me to get an abortion."

"Damn, Koda. When you found out you was pregnant? You was drinking and shit yesterday."

"The drinks don't matter because I'm not having Maleek's baby. It'll permanently tie me to him and I can't go back to that!" She exclaimed before bursting into a fit of tears. I paused for a moment then gently rubbed her back as she choked through the rest of her statement. "I was really horny; my nipples felt super sensitive when you touched them last night. Then when I threw up yesterday morning, it was like everything hit me at once."

"Stop crying, Koda. I got you, now, always and forever. Whatever you need, I got you," I pulled her into a tight hug.

Koda exhaled deeply, pulling her shirt up to clean her face. "I promise I was going to call you. I found out yesterday after I left your house. I never get stomach sick like that and I was having headaches last week and my period is four days late so I took a test. My parents will not condone in me getting an abortion and I drove myself to my first appointment yesterday, but apparently you have to have two appointments before they will give you the pills. When I woke up both of my parents and their cars were gone and they won't be back anytime soon."

"You don't have to explain, I told you I got you. What time is your appointment?"

"In an hour but we can leave now because I can't afford for anything to happen and I miss this appointment. They called me because they had a cancellation, my appointment was originally going to be next week."

"Get yo shit so we can go," I encouraged.

Koda went into her bedroom for a moment and returned with her purse a few moments later. This was a new experience for me. I never knew what went down at abortion clinics because I stayed rubbered up. Last thing I needed was one of these hoes tied to me by a kid for the rest of my life. Glancing at Koda, I wouldn't mind being tied to her for eternity.

"That's the clinic?" I questioned, noticing the angry mob of people holding signs in front of the building.

"Unfortunately, there were even more people out here ready to mind other people's business yesterday," Koda rolled her eyes. "Just ignore them and keep walking."

I hit the gas and crossed the intersection then turned into the parking lot of the clinic. Like flies on shit, they were ready to come preach to some motha fuckas who didn't want to hear shit they had to say.

"I'mma come open your door, don't get out yet," I informed Koda and she nodded her head.

Killing the engine, I rounded the car and opened the door so Koda could get out. As we walked towards the entrance these motha fuckas started off chill. Saying shit like, there were other options and they could help her explore them, but it seemed like they got aggressive since we collectively ignored them without breaking our stride.

"You're walking into the devil's den! Repent for your sins!"

"Abortion is murder! You'll answer to God for this if you don't turn away now!"

"God condemns those who shed innocent blood! Turn away from this wickedness!" A few of them shouted and I was over the shit.

"Yeah, yeah, yeah. That wig should be condemned," I spat at the woman with a big ass *abortion is murder* sign. Her mouth fell open like she was shocked, but I know she saw that ugly shit when she looked in the mirror this morning.

"Your child deserves a chance at life! Don't take away their God-given right! Face your duties head-on and be a man, take charge of your responsibilities! You were both mature enough to engage in creating life; now it's time to mature further and take responsibility for that life!" She argued.

"Bruh, it's not even my baby," I laughed. "But I did fuck her last night. Nutting all on the baby head and shit. I think we both can agree this ain't the type of life the baby needs."

"Jax," Koda shrieked.

I took my eyes off of the woman momentarily to look at Koda and when I looked back up this bitch grabbed something out of her purse and flicked some liquid on us. I snatched the shit out of her hand and launched it across the parking lot. My actions must've angered one of the men in the crowd because she pushed his bitch ass forward holding a sign and damn near touched Koda.

Over these simple motha fuckas, I pulled my gun off my waist and moved it from side to side so they all got a good look. "Move the fuck around before I start dumping. Then all you bitches can babysit the aborted babies in the afterlife. Out here minding business that doesn't pertain to you! I spent some time in the foster care system, one of those *other options* y'all talking about and that shit ain't pretty."

They scattered like roaches and I quickly led Koda inside of the clinic.

"Are you guys okay?" The receptionist inquired as we approached the door she was holding open. "I don't know what's wrong with them, they are getting more hostile."

"Yeah, well they had the right one today," I explained, looking out of the window to see they were nowhere in sight. "They better stay gone until we leave. I told you I'm always going to make sure you straight," I assured Koda before kissing her forehead.

She smiled and snuggled into my side as we approached the receptionist desk. I missed this shit, I don't care if it was only a little over a day, she had a nigga fiending for her and shit. Clearly I was fucked up about Koda and nothing was going to change that. Right or wrong, I was on whatever behind her.

KODA

Four Days Later

Since taking the pills, I spent my time curled up in the bed next to Jax. I wasn't heartless, the abortion had my emotions all over the place, but I knew it was best for me and my unfortunate situation. Looking at myself in the mirror after brushing my teeth, I told myself it was for the best before tip-toeing to the door and trying to open it without making any noise.

"Where the fuck you going?" Jax asked as I tried to slip out of the bedroom, but the creaky ass door woke him up. "I sleep light as fuck, stop trying to be sneaky."

"I was trying to cook you breakfast to thank you for taking such good care of me.

The cramping finally subsided last night and I was up moving around against Jax's wishes. Despite the doctor's assurance that I could resume normal activities the day after ingesting the second pill, he insisted on catering to my every need, waiting on me hand and foot. I wasn't complaining either, the cramps and bleeding were beating my ass the first three days. Now I just felt like the third or fourth day of my period.

"You don't have to do that," Jax assured me, peeling himself out of the bed.

Watching as he approached me, I would never get over how good his embrace felt. I tucked myself into his arms and he pulled me back towards the bed. "You need to lay down and call your parents. Ma called me last night talking shit about me stealing you away from them," he explained.

"Oh you calling her ma now?"

"Why wouldn't I?"

"No reason," I grinned as my phone rang.

"Go ahead and get that, it can only be one of them. You want french toast?"

"Yes, I'll take french toast," I confirmed before grabbing my phone. "Hey ma, hey dad," I chirped into the phone.

"Why haven't we seen you since you snuck out of here like four days ago?" My mom badgered before leaning closer to the phone to whisper. "Are you laid up with Jax?"

"Cali, I'm sitting right here, I can hear you," my dad shook his head at her.

"Well close your ears or something, Kyle."

She peeled herself off the bed and walked out of their room and into the living room to sit on the couch. "Stop lying to me Koda, I just want to know what's going on between y'all."

"Ma, you like super nosey," I chuckled, walking into the bathroom to wash my face.

"I just want to know what's going on," she sassed, tilting her head to the side with her face screwed up.

"I don't know what's going on, ma."

"Mhhhh hmmmm," she huffed as I rubbed the face wash into my skin.

"What kind of fruit you want me to put on your plate?" Jax questioned from behind me in the bathroom door and my mom's eyes immediately darted in his direction.

"Jax, what's going on with y'all."

"Ion know ma," Jax laughed. "I told you that when you called last night."

"Y'all sound like some damn parrots. Ion know, ma." She grumbled, waving us off as I rinsed my face.

"As soon as we know we will let you know," I interrupted their exchange and turned to Jax. "I want some of those mangos, they were so good yesterday."

"Alright."

Jax walked off and I redirected my attention to my phone while patting my face dry. "Well, I don't care what y'all got going on but make sure you bring your ass over here while I'm off work. I sent you my schedule."

"I'll look at your schedule and confirm the time after I eat breakfast."

"I'll be waiting. I love you."

"I love you too," I cooed before disconnecting the call.

Exiting the bathroom, I took a seat on the bed and dialed my office number. It had been eight days since I left, and it took everything out of me to refrain from calling my team. Although I reviewed my business accounts yesterday and confirmed that payroll went out as expected, I still needed to check in with them, and let them know what was going on. The truth was, I hadn't successfully gotten Maleek to sign the documents relinquishing his co-owner status. He had the lawyers, money, and business acumen to hold my business against me since he knew I took off with Jax. After planning my speech, I built the courage to hit the call button.

"Thank you for calling Stellar Financial Services, this is Michelle, how may I help you today?" Michelle greeted me and I could feel her smile through the phone.

"Hey Michelle, it's Koda..."

"Kodaaaaaaa!" Michelle exclaimed before I could complete my sentence. "Girrrrrrl, we have been worried sick about yo ass. Maleek's face was all over the news for his arrest last Friday, then the next morning his lawyer was holding a press conference saying he was a victim of police brutality and shit. I was blowing your phone up and I stopped by your house on Sunday. Don't worry, we running shit but worried nonetheless. Shit, I was scared you were caught up with Maleek's bullshit but we didn't see a mugshot for you."

"No, no mugshots over here, and I'm fine, but I had to leave. I needed some time to myself."

"Koda, you don't have to fake the funk in front of me. This is a judgment free zone. I'll forever be grateful for you putting me in the position I'm in. If you running from that nigga stay gone. Maleek was released from police custody today and the news said he should be discharged from the hospital today."

"Are you serious?" I fretted, not expecting to hear that. The way Simone was talking I just knew Maleek would be in there for some serious time.

"As a heart attack," Michelle confirmed.

"Well I'm glad I called. I hate to do this to y'all but Maleek is the co-owner and he may try to make things hard for y'all. If he happens to come there asking about me please don't tell him you talked to me and absolutely don't give him my number. You can call me if anything goes down, but on some real shit, y'all might need to start looking for backup jobs and print out hard copies of your client lists, just in case he was to do some shiesty shit like lock y'all out and take your company laptops," I detailed.

"I'm already a step ahead of you. I had everybody export contacts and other things once we saw that you were MIA. We ready for whatever, don't worry about us. You have to do what's best for you. Oh shit girl. I've had a client sitting in the waiting room and I'm steady yapping my gums. I'll call you back if anything pops off," Michelle panicked.

"Okay. I appreciate you!"

"We appreciate you too. Bye."

She hung up and Jax entered the room carrying two plates. "I could've sat at the table today," I snipped.

"Nah, we relaxing in the bed for one more day, Dr. Jax's orders."

"No can do, I already told my mom that I was coming over before she goes to work," I argued, taking my plate.

"Oh yeah, we can go to see ma and pops any day of the week."

"I also need to go car shopping so you don't have to play taxi all of the time."

"What else I gotta do?" He shrugged then slid a slice of mango in his mouth.

"Do you know how fine you are?" I questioned, genuinely gawking over his fine ass.

"The hoes be screaming that shit but it only matters when it comes from you," he leaned over and kissed my lips. I'd never get enough of that.

"But for real, I gotta find a car. What am I going to do when you leave?" I tossed out there, wanting desperately for him to refute the assertion but he didn't.

"I guess that makes sense. You'll have to get around," he nodded.

"Yep, have you figured out when you're leaving yet?"

"Nah, just playing shit by ear. Told you I was waiting on my man with the boat. Trying to disappear like a thief in the night."

"*More like the thief with my heart.*" I thought to myself before digging into my plate.

MALEEK

"Thank you for uncuffing my client," Chad smiled smugly at the officer on duty.

After the hearing this morning, I was no longer in police custody while I waited on the grand jury to decide whether or not they were going to indict me. Chad was confident that the charges would be dropped due to lack of evidence, but until then I wasn't allowed to leave the state. Koda and Jax were probably already out of the country somewhere since they had an eight day head start, and that young nigga was strategic. The thought of them two walking out of my house with my go bag in hand, almost sent me into a blind rage at least once a day since I've been in here. The moment the cuff slipped off my arm, the sense of freedom consumed me for the first time in days.

"Thanks officer," I nodded, grabbing my discharge papers and exiting the hospital.

Fuck the procedures of getting wheeled out, I had shit to do. Couldn't be waiting around for these slow ass nurses to do shit for me. Chad marched out behind me, talking low enough for my ears only as I tapped the button for the elevator.

"Maleek, whatever you do, don't get arrested again. We have a great lawsuit in the works, and your charges are going to be dropped. Don't do anything to add more drama onto my plate."

I ignored his ass and stepped through the opening doors. Once we were on the elevator and the door shut, I invaded his space and fear instantly flashed across his face. "Chad, don't worry about what the fuck I do. You worry about getting these charges dropped and finding out where the fuck Koda is."

"I got ya boss. My guy tracked her phone and it's back at your house. She didn't take any electronics with her and she hasn't used any money from her bank accounts," he explained. "As far as Jax, you know he was very meticulous like you. I don't know where he kept his money but it won't be traceable by us or the US government."

"Yeah, because she ran off with a million dollars cash, she don't need shit else," I snarled, punching the elevator wall behind him.

There was plenty more where that came from, it wasn't the money that had me stressing, it was losing Koda to Jax that had me out of body. That intense sense of anger consumed me as I thought about how long they were fucking around behind my back. I should've known they had something going on when he came to her rescue in the kitchen that day. On that day, I was thinking the nigga was so sensitive because his mama used to get her ass beat like a fucking piñata.

However, Jax came back to get Koda after what went down at the warehouse. I should've known better, I couldn't blame anybody but my damn self. The lil nigga was in love with my bitch when they were in high school, I was lacking for being so laxed and letting him around her.

"Give me your fucking keys!" I demanded as my impulses consumed me. Simone had answers and she was about to cough them bitches up.

"Give you my keys?" Chad spluttered in shock.

"Give me the fucking keys," I gripped his neck and squeezed tightly, pushing him into the wall.

Chad fumbled around in his pockets before producing the keys. The elevator dinged and I released the grip I had on his weak ass. My fucking sides were throbbing from using my muscles to jack his ass up.

I coughed and that shit shot pain everywhere as I marched out of the hospital. Holding Chad's key fob in the air, I clicked the button and his whip beeped on the left side of the parking lot until I finally found it.

Twenty minutes later I swerved into the driveway of Simone's house and her cheap ass Beemer was in the driveway. Stupid ass bitch had her curtains drawn and I could see her sitting on her couch all smiles while putting her dog on the leash.

"*I'm here right on time*," I mumbled to myself. With no guns in sight and a body that was still sore as fuck from the ass whooping the police put on me, I couldn't shoot or kick the door down. Standing on the porch, I greeted Simone with a bright smile as she opened the door with her Shih Tzu in hand.

"Maleek!" Simone shrieked, eyes the size of dinner plates. She dropped the dog causing him to yelp out when he collided with the floor. The lil nigga barked at me and I swiftly kicked his ass across the room.

HARF! HARF! HARF!

He cried out before hitting the wall and running his scary ass in the opposite direction. Simone tried to run but I yanked her ass back by the hair. Her natural tresses were pulled into a high bun and I wrapped it around my hand once, getting a good grip on her shit. Stepping inside, I slammed the door behind me and her wall decor shook.

"I checked Koda's call record and yo bitch ass was the last person she talked to, so I know you know where she is," I explained.

"I… I…" Simone stuttered and I yanked her ass around so we were face to face. I needed this bitch to understand I wasn't fucking around.

"It wasn't a question, it was a statement. I know you talked to her last so just tell me where the fuck did her and Jax go?"

"Jax?" Simone questioned.

"Don't act dumb, I know you knew they were messing around."

"I swear I don't know what you're talking about," Simone cried.

"Where the fuck they at, Simone?!" I roared and next thing I know, this bitch kneed me in the stomach.

Intense pain surged through every part of my body, causing me to double over in agony. That gave Simone a minute to run while I tried to gather my bearings. "Georgie!" She called out and I heard that stupid ass dog rushing towards her. I got my shit together and moved in their direction, stepping on the leash trailing the dog. Simone lifted a can of mace and sprayed that shit all in my face.

"AGHHHHHH!" I screamed, lifting my shirt to wipe my eyes.

I knew her kitchen was straight ahead and I rushed in that direction, knocking shit over, causing myself more pain. It took me a minute to find the sink and when I did, the water didn't seem to help my fight against the harsh chemicals. ***Milk!*** I thought to myself and felt around until I found her refrigerator and poured milk all in my eyes.

"I'mma kill that bitch too!" My voice echoed into the lonely home because Simone was long gone. I heard her and that dog rush out the backdoor while I was drowning my eyes in water.

It took me a minute to calm myself to depart Simone's house but I knew the bitch may call the cops or her brother, so I had to get the fuck on. Plus I had other shit to accomplish today as well. I pulled out of Simone's driveway and went home to change out of my milk soaked hoodie and joggers that my parents grabbed for me while I was in the hospital. Once I woke up and had them run a few errands for me, I sent their ass back to Atlanta. They wasn't fucking with me before the police stomped me out and there was no need to come along now with all that preaching. Plus, I saw the look of approval in my parents eyes when I told them Koda left me. They been wanted her to get the fuck away from me, so they could move around to.

Two hours later I pulled up to Stellar Financial Services. With my gun tucked on my waist, I swaggered through the glass doors in a three piece suit and the first office I could see into was Michelle's. Our gazes locked and her smug ass was on the phone; she instantly rolled her eyes and sat the phone down on the receiver. There was a second set of glass doors I walked through to enter her office.

"Hello, how may I help you?" Michelle greeted me, not bothering to hide her disdain as I plopped into the leather chair across from her.

"Ion know much about what goes on in here, but I know Koda always leaves you in charge if she is out of office so I'll ask this once. Do you know where Koda is?

"No," she answered and I couldn't read her at all.

"Have you talked to her since she took off last Friday?"

"No one in the office has heard from her but we still have a job to do so we are here," she shrugged. "Is everything okay?"

"Nah, you're fired, gather your shit and get the fuck up out of here and leave the company issued devices behind," I commanded.

"What you expect me to beg? Fuck you and this job," she spat, grabbing her purse from her desk drawer. "Them police should've killed yo no good ass."

"What?" I hopped from my seat and she pulled the lil baby pistol she mentioned before from her purse.

Laughing at that shit, I shrugged. "That shit don't scare me, you got five minutes to be gone."

Sauntering out of her office, I went to the next door and opened it. Looked like all of the other employees were in here watching TikToks, having a good ass time on the clock. "You motha fuckas are all fired! Get y'all shit and get the fuck up out of here! You got five minutes!" I interrupted their good time, leaving their jaws on the floor. Tapping my Rolex, I exited the office and marched down the hallway until I reached the door that had Koda's name on a gold placard. Starting with the file cabinet against the wall, I rummaged through her files. No matter how long it took, Koda was coming home.

JAX

Two Weeks Later

Around nine o'clock this morning, I dropped Koda off at her parents' house to go shopping with her mom before she had to go to work at the spa. Unbeknownst to Koda, I slipped her mom a few dollars to make sure Koda grabbed bathing suits for the both of us because I had a surprise for her when she got back. Pushing the Publix cart through the chip aisle, I grabbed a box of assorted chips before moving on to grab the subs I ordered online. While waiting in the ten item or less line, I spotted a picnic basket and grabbed that as well. My phone vibrated and it was a text from Koda letting me know they were on their way back to the crib, so I put a little pep in my step.

Koda loved the sun and warm weather since we came to Florida, but we hadn't made it to the beach yet. Every time we put the beach on our agenda, the weather thwarted our plans with a thunderstorm. Mrs. Allen told me to start checking the weather daily and that's what I did. With clear skies in the forecast Koda would finally have her beach day.

All she kept telling Mrs. Allen was how back in Alabama we didn't have a beach and the closest thing we had was Alabama Water Adventure. A water park that neither of us went to in years. Now we were a twenty minute drive from Clearwater beach. Although Mrs. Allen suggested I take Koda to Siesta Key beach that was over an hour away. I was willing to take that drive to give Koda the best experience. Shit, we explored restaurants from Clearwater to Orlando, and anywhere in between, whenever Koda came across something on TikTok. She wasn't above long drives for a good time. Seeing her smile, displaying all of her teeth, always made a nigga feel more human again, so I was down too.

When I made it home, I took the groceries in the house and washed my hands to prepare the picnic basket. We had subs, a fruit and veggie tray, and chips. By the time I was done Koda was keying in the passcode and entering the house.

"What's this?" She questioned, entering the kitchen with an arm full of bags from various stores.

"A picnic basket for us to take to the beach," I replied, leaning in to peck her lips.

"So that's why my mama insisted that I buy new bathing suits? I swear it feels like she likes you more than me sometimes," Koda frowned her face up.

"Stop hating on me and my girl and go get changed. Where my shit at so I can get dressed too?"

"Say less because you know I've been wanting to go to the beach real bad. I'll leave your trunks on the bed."

Koda strutted out the kitchen as I grabbed the bottles of water from the freezer and sat them near the fruit to help keep them cold. Closing the picnic basket, I headed to the bedroom and offered Koda a mean mug once I saw the bright orange swim trunks she bought me.

"I guess I should've told mama to get black trunks. We about to be out here looking like a pair of tangerines," I laughed because her orange bathing suit matched mine.

"Shut up," she giggled, spinning around and backing up towards me so I could tie her top.

"You so fucking fine," I expressed, leaning down to plant a kiss on her shoulder adorned with a huge tattoo of Mother Earth sporting dreads and a massive gold crown while cradling her stomach, featuring the Earth at its center. The rest of her sleeve showcased a beautiful array of detailed flowers. Every time she exposed her tattoos, I couldn't resist kissing them; the shit was sexy as fuck. They stood in stark contrast to mine, which depicted a more ruthless nature – portraits of my late mother and brother, a ski mask, AK-47s, and various dark art pieces adorned my body.

"Don't start," she giggled, pulling away after I placed countless kisses. "I'm trying to make it to the beach."

"Alright, let me slip this bright shit on so we can go. Yo mama told me to take you to Siesta Key beach and they don't let you reserve the cabanas so we need to get there before they are all gone."

"I'm ready," she explained, slipping her bottoms on.

I changed into my swim trunks, slid on my slides, then grabbed our picnic basket and mini cooler before stepping out of the house. Koda alternated between completing sudoku puzzles, and singing her heart out to the playlist she picked during the drive. When we got there I carried the cooler and Koda grabbed the picnic basket while we went through the process of renting the cabana. We ate a little of the food and quickly learned how aggressive the Florida birds were before finding our way to the water.

I would've preferred to sit underneath the cabana, but whatever Koda wanted, she got. We were waist-deep in the water, the gentle waves crashing against our lower abdomen as we stared into the endless water. Children laughing, water splashing, and distant chatter made this shit serene. Holding Koda from behind, I leaned in and kissed her neck.

"You know, back in high school, I had the biggest crush on you," I grinned, mentally reminiscing on the past. I felt her tilt up to look at me and I looked down.

"I had my suspicions," Koda expressed.

"Yeah, I tried to keep the shit under wraps, only told Maleek, Randal, and Kenneth. They all told me to step down on you, but I never did. Then after Kenneth passed away you was fucking with Maleek, and I was in the midst of grief, so it was just like big ups to my nigga."

"Wow, that adds another layer to Maleek's treachery. Makes me wonder if that's what made him notice and try to pursue me. He's fucking sick," Koda commented, before turning around to wrap her arms around my neck and kiss me passionately.

"He did a lot of dirt but we survived, and it led us to each other, and I feel like this is where we were meant to be."

"Facts," I smiled, leaning down to scoop Koda off of her feet and dunk her ass in the water.

"Jaaaaaaax!" She squealed as I rushed towards the shore as she tossed water at my back.

It was difficult running out of the water and I felt her lil ass dive on me, wrapping her arms around my legs to take me down. I fell underneath the shallow water and pulled her ass under with me. Wrapping my arm around Koda's back, I pulled her up so she was on top of me and planted a kiss on her lips as the waves crashed into us. I was falling and bad as fuck too.

After a few hours, we packed up and took the long drive home because I had one more trick up my sleeve for the day. Once we showered and redressed, I interrupted Koda in the living room talking to her mom on the phone.

"Come on, it's time to go car shopping."

"Yesssssss, did you see the Honda I sent you online?" She questioned me before redirecting her attention to her mom on the phone. "I gotta call you back, I'm about to go look at cars. I love you." Koda disconnected the call and hopped to her feet, waiting for my answer.

"Yeah, we can take a look at that first," I suggested as Koda grabbed her bags.

We left the house and made it to US-19 where it seemed like all the car lots were located but I didn't stop at the Honda dealership like I initially suggested.

"No Jax, I said I wanted a lowkey car now," Koda whined as we pulled into Ferman BMW.

"Shut that shit up and relax. I'm getting you whatever the fuck I wanna get you," I smiled at her.

"No, I'm for real, Jax." Koda sat up in her seat and turned in my direction once I placed the car in park. "I was in an abusive relationship so I know that some men don't mean no harm when they do things like that but it has a double meaning for me. I want to pick out my own car, I want to be in control and I need you to understand that. I didn't even pick the AMG I used to drive, of course I grew to love it, but I always wanted a lil Benz coupe."

The resonance of Koda's words echoed deep within me. There weren't any controlling intentions behind my previous statement; I just wanted to buy Koda something nice and she was fighting me on it. However, I respected her position and her wish was my command.

"Alright, to the Honda dealership we go. You want a Honda Accord, I'mma get that but I'm buying you the newest model and adding all the extra shit," I assured her before leaning over to kiss her cheek.

Koda gripped the sides of my face and planted her lips on mine. I swear her lips always felt like the gateway to heaven, they were naturally soft and luscious. Then include the cocoa-flavored lip gloss, which I'm convinced should be classified as an aphrodisiac, and I wanted to do more than kiss. I wanted to dip my dick deep inside her guts while she screamed my name and drug her nails across my back.

"Thank you," Koda bubbled once we broke the kiss.

I paused to settle my hormones before reversing out of the parking spot. "You know I can get you that lil coupe you always wanted," I interrupted the silence.

Koda smirked, placing her finger on her chin as we waited for an opportunity to join traffic on the highway. "I can compromise with that," she bubbled.

"Say less," I grinned, redirecting the GPS.

The dealership was only ten minutes south of where we were. Upon entering the dealership we were assisted by a black woman named Patina who might've been in her mid to late twenties. Koda didn't have a clue what the fuck she wanted but I silently trailed behind her as she figured it out. This bipolar ass weather had the sun beating down on us today and Koda was wearing shorts, a white cami and a pair of panda Dunks. Shorts and sneakers were her bag when the weather was hot, and joggers were her shit when it was cold. Either way, she always looked good as fuck. All of her tattoos were on display again and I loved that shit, when we were undressed her body mirrored mine, how could I not admire it?

When she saw an E 450 Coupe she looked up at me with a huge smile on her face. "Jax, this is the one," she chirped, bouncing over to me. I wrapped my arm around Koda's back and she leaned up to plant a kiss on my lips.

"Y'all are the cutest couple," Patina complimented. She was doing that throughout the entire interaction and I loved hearing it. I felt complete with Koda by my side.

"Thank you," Koda smiled at her.

"Would you guys like to take it for a test drive?"

"Yes, please." Koda grinned.

"Let me go grab the keys."

Patina disappeared inside of the building and when she returned Koda got in the driver's seat and I sat in the back. We took a short ride and Koda loved it, you couldn't pay her to wipe the smile off of her face, so I told Patina to get the paperwork started for a cash deal. Sitting in a small office with Patina while we waited on whatever they had to do to get us out of the door, Koda's phone rang. My eyes landed on the phone as well because that was the first time her phone rang since she got it.

"It's my employee Michelle, I gotta take this," Koda excused herself.

"So what do you two do?" Patina pried after a minute or two of silence.

My eyes were still locked on Koda as she conversed on the phone outside. It was the glass offices that allowed me to relax while she stepped out alone. Anything related to Koda and Birmingham didn't sit well with me.

"A lot," I kept shit brief. My business didn't have shit to do with her, all I wanted was the keys and title so I could get the fuck on.

"Would you mind elaborating on that?"

"The fuck is you, the Feds or something?" I whipped my head in her direction.

"No," she chuckled. "You just don't see many people who can come in here and drop cash on a car." Now that I was looking at Patina, her eyes lingered on me for too long, and her smile became more sugges- tive before she opened her mouth to speak again. "Not trying to be in your business, just trying to see if I can get in where I fit in. With that type of cash you can afford more than one woman," she flirted, biting her bottom lip.

"Nah man," I laughed, sitting back in my seat to text Koda.

Me: You better come back. She trying to "get in where she fit in" her words. (crying laughing emoji)

I kept my eyes on Koda as she read the text before ending the call and marching back in our direction. The door swung open, and Koda pranced in with her face screwed up. "Girl hurry the fuck up with this paperwork. If you would've flirted with my last nigga I would've gladly handed him over but about this one I'll cause a scene and get yo ass fired. Get yo silly ass up, you think everything fucking funny," Koda directed her last sentence at me.

"Nah, they already got my money, I ain't leaving this office until we got them keys."

"How much longer is this supposed to take," Koda questioned Patina and I loved seeing her react over a nigga. The other night she was talking about me leaving, had a nigga thinking I was just dick for the moment.

"Let me go check on the paperwork for you guys," she stated before exiting the office.

"She probably have her ass in here flirting with any nigga that got a lil money and you like the shit huh?" Koda sassed.

"Nah, I only like you," I expressed, pulling her down in my lap while I stared into her bright eyes. No matter the bullshit Koda went through, she didn't let it break her. "You like a nigga huh? I wasn't sure."

"Why would you ask that?"

"Shit, you asked me when I was leaving like you didn't give a fuck the other night."

"It wasn't that I didn't give a fuck, I wasn't trying to hold you back. Your plan seemed so elaborate that I wasn't sure if you'd reconsider for me."

"I'm falling for you, Koda," I confessed.

"I'm falling for you too," Koda replied, kissing my lips.

"We gone do this for real? Once you make that commitment there ain't no turning back, I ain't never coming up off you."

The door swung open and Patina entered with an older white man and Koda's keys. "You guys are all set to go, we appreciate your business and I hope that we will see you guys again in the future."

"You gotta watch that one, she's a little flirty," Koda snickered, grabbing the keys to her car as we exited the dealership.

I trailed her outside and the car was parked right out front for her. After sharing another kiss, Koda climbed in her new whip and drove off. I walked to the Honda and took off too. With a moment to myself on our way back to the Airbnb, I did my daily legal check to see if Maleek had any changes in his status as an inmate. Seeing released on bond, I knew Chad's bitch ass could tell me what I really needed to know. Switching my sim cards, I placed a call to the grimy ass white boy who I should've known would always have Maleek's back before he had mine. Chad was our lawyer, we did business together for years and he helped us keep our hands clean. The difference was, I had dirt on Chad that even Maleek didn't know about.

"This is attorney Chad," he answered in his professional voice.

"This is Jax, and Chad you know what the fuck I want. Did that nigga work a deal?" I questioned.

"I can't breech client-attorney confidentiality," he whined like the bitch he was.

"Do you know what it would be like if I stuck my nine in your mouth and pulled the trigger for you not informing me that Maleek was going to snitch on me? You were both of our lawyers but do you really want me to be the one who feels like you betrayed him?"

"Jax, I..."

"Before you lie," I cut him off. "I overheard you on the phone with Maleek. He was ready to throw me to the Feds and you was going to let him. That tells me you was gone help the bitch ass nigga. Now wassup? You trying to taste this steel or I got one better. I could make it public how I helped you run your competition out of Birmingham. I vividly remember a few years back when you were losing clients to a new slick talking lawyer and you asked for a favor. I had no problem breaking his leg and telling him to get out of town if he knew what was best for him. He left too and the police never knew who attacked him but I can bring some new evidence to the light."

"Alright, what do you want to know Jax?"

"I just want to know if he's talking, what he's saying and how I factor into all of this?"

"You haven't heard?"

"How the fuck am I going to hear some shit when I'm out of the city and not speaking with anyone?"

"In the simplest way possible, the warehouse was empty, the house and restaurants were clean, and the police beat Maleek to a pulp so he is looking at having the charges dropped while we file a lawsuit against BPD. In fact, some civil rights attorneys are even looking at coming to Birmingham to prop him up as a victim of senseless police brutality. You guys don't have anything to worry about. Maleek didn't have to tell on anyone and for the record, when Maleek suggested turning you in I told him that would be the dumbest thing. They would still hand him a harsh sentence even if he pinned everything on you. No prosecutor or grand jury was going to believe that he was working for you, a man ten years his junior. Your name was never brought up and from the evidence I saw they have no idea who you are, Maleek was their target."

"Has he been looking for Koda?"

"I think you know the answer to that," he shot back. "But nobody has found anything. Koda is one hundred percent off the grid."

"Even if one of your PI's find something, make it disappear or your ass will be a dead man walking."

"I got you Jax, my lips are sealed. This conversation never happened and I don't know anything about Koda's whereabouts."

"Good."

I disconnected the call, unsure of how I felt at that moment. Just a few minutes ago, I was all about seeing where shit could go with Koda, but now I had other shit on my mind. The thought of our operation, the one thing I was good at, reverting back to Maleek's hand to reap the benefits alone didn't sit right with me. Mindlessly driving the rest of the way to the crib, I pulled up behind Koda and ran my hands over my face, preparing to tuck my internal debate before entering the house.

"I love love love it," Koda bubbled, snuggling up into my arms once I stepped out of the car.

"I'm happy you do," I offered a fake ass smile, wrapping my arms around her.

We entered the house and Koda's mom was calling to talk about her new whip. When they got on the phone they cackled like a pair of hyenas talking about everything under the sun. I'm sure that Maleek thought time and distance would diminish their relationship but it seemed to do the opposite. Lacking both parents myself, witnessing Koda's happiness with her own always warmed a nigga's cold heart. I gave them space to talk their shit and went into the room to get my own thoughts together.

If their case was in the toilet, Birmingham was calling a nigga, but taking Koda back with me was out of the question. I was determined to keep her far away from that nigga Maleek, and I couldn't separate her from her parents again. My mind was running a mile a minute as my heart pulled me in two different directions. On one hand, I caught feelings for Koda and she had a nigga head fucked up, and on the other was my love for the game. That was my one and only love in life up until this point.

Maleek couldn't run Birmingham without me by his side, it took this incident for me to realize that. Niggas feared me, niggas respected me, and that's why the moment I was gone they ran off with all of that nigga's shit. I wouldn't trust them niggas again, once a thief, always a thief, but I could rebuild. Laying back in the bed, I placed both hands behind my head and stared up at the ceiling, silently making plays to rebuild my shit and wipe Maleek off the map.

I was deep in my thoughts too because I didn't even hear Koda come into the room. She bounced on the bed and straddled me. When I looked up, a smile spread across my face because she was dressed in a black lingerie set.

"I went to see my new gynecologist today and she said I'm clear for some freaky shit," Koda grinned down at me.

Looking up at her, I admired every detail on her beautiful face but

I couldn't look her in the eyes. Gently caressing her thighs, I redirected my gaze towards the ceiling. "What's wrong with you?" Koda inquired. She repositioned herself so her knees were near my side and her hands were planted next to my shoulders, so her goofy ass was looking me in my eyes.

"Talking to my old lawyer and the fairytale I was living in is over."

"What does that mean?" Koda questioned, with a scowl on her pretty face.

"Maleek getting off on the charges and that means my name isn't in the mix and since it was never in the mix I can go back to handle my business."

Koda grimaced, sitting up, folding her arms across her chest with her bottom lip poked out. "Why would you do that?"

"I didn't put in all of that work to let Maleek reap all of the benefits."

"So you expect me to go back to Birmingham and what? Hide out for eternity?"

"Nah, I would never ask you to do that because..."

"So you just about to leave me?" Koda cut me off, her frown deepening.

"No, you deserve better than that, Koda. Hell, you deserve better than me or anything I can give you. There isn't anything I wouldn't do for you. But I'mma keep shit G, I'mma always be a dope boy, I ain't got shit else going for me. I faked my way into a GED by paying some nigga to take the test for me so I could get the lil certificate but Ion have shit else. All I've known since I was what... sixteen years old, is the dope game. Ion have no work history, didn't spend the last few years in college or no shit like that, all I got is what I left in Birmingham. I know you see me in a different light, I'm this sweet ass nigga since we been here but money, murder, and the dope game is what made me."

I expressed honestly sitting up in the bed. Placing my hand on Koda's waist, I was about to move her off me so I could get up. Her gaze was intimidating, I saw the heartbreak in her eyes and the shit was fucking me up. Before I could move her, Koda cupped my chin and forced me to meet her gaze.

"Since we've been here I've had some hard honest conversations with my mom. I realize that I was groomed by Maleek and I feel like he groomed you to think negatively about yourself, just like he did to me. It took a lot for me to believe that I was worth so much more than Maleek was giving me in our relationship. When you cupped my face in the kitchen and told me that I deserved more that day I believed it. I could feel it in your tone, the sincerity was clear in your eyes. I hope that you can see the same things in mine because I mean it when I say you're more than a shooter, a dope boy, or a street nigga. If you can run a multimillion dollar drug organization while evading the law then you can run a business. The world deserves everything you have to offer. You had no business doing whatever Maleek had you doing in that year that you disappeared after Kenneth's murder. You just need to take time to think about what you like to do, what you're good at and go from there. When I took that call from Michelle earlier she informed me that last week Maleek came in and fired everyone so my business is ruined, there is no saving it. But you know what, I am okay with that. I'm throwing in the towel with my business back home and I have an interview at a financial firm here tomorrow. We can start over and figure this out together. It won't be easy but it'll be worth it. We're stronger together, Jax."

Koda's lecture hit somewhere deep in my soul because she was right. Those seeds were implanted in my head since the day he got me out of the foster home after my brother's death. At the young impressionable age of sixteen, Maleek's word was the gospel and it had a hold on me until the moment I witnessed him putting his hands on Koda. I knew he wasn't the man I thought he was, then add in the fact that he was ready to snitch on me, and I realized he was never the man I thought he was. I hadn't experienced anyone speaking life into me since my brother died and the shit had me about to shed a few thug tears. Koda didn't know how much I needed her, how bad I needed to hear that shit. Closing my eyes, I placed my forehead against Koda's and she released the grip she had on my shit. She gripped both of my hands, and I felt our connection deepen in that moment. I believed Koda, we could do this.

"I love you, Koda," I confessed before kissing her passionately.

Those words hadn't left my lips in years but this was definitely love. Had to be, if I was ready to throw in the towel and walk away from the dope game.

Feeling the weight of those three words, I gripped Koda's hair and pulled her ponytail out. Tasting the faint cocoa from her lips as she grinded into my lap, I deepened the kiss, trying to express my feelings through the motions of my tongue. Pulling Koda's head back with the grip on her ponytail, I trailed my kisses down her neck and used my free hand to massage her right breast through the thin piece of lace.

"Fuck, Jax!" Koda moaned in pleasure.

My mouth followed my hand's path moments later, kissing her nipples through the lace before pulling the fabric down. I alternated sucking and squeezing her titties with my left hand while my right hand found their way between her legs. Her pussy was already leaking through the fabric allowing my fingers to slip right in. Looking up at Koda biting her lips, I loved every moment of sex with her nasty ass. She grinded into my fingers before leaning down to kiss me tenderly.

"Stop teasing me Jax, give me that dick," she commanded.

My dick was crying in my shorts as Koda frantically fumbled with the single button. I pulled my finger out of Koda to help her out and the moment my dick was released, she pushed me back on the bed, and held the base while slowly slipping down on this big motha fucka.

"Go 'head bae, take all this dick," I encouraged. Closing my eyes, I reveled in the feeling I missed bad as fuck. I only got the pussy for one night before the abortion put us on restrictions. Her shit was sloppy wet and I felt her juices dripping down my balls. Koda leaned down to kiss me while bouncing on my dick before placing her hands on the headboard to help her ride me with precision. Bouncing up and down, she was moaning louder than the macaroni sounds bouncing off the walls. Reaching up, I caressed her nipples, watching her take all this dick with her wet ass pussy did something to a nigga.

"This dick so good, Jax! You trying to take it away from me?"

"Never, bae," I groaned, sitting up so we were eye to eye as I gripped her hips and bounced her up and down.

"Promise?" She cried out.

"Promise, Koda."

"I'mma cum, Jax. Fuck me just like that!"

I leaned in and sucked her neck while I felt her walls convulsing on my dick. Her pussy fit me so good that her orgasm pulled the nut out of me every time and I was savoring the moment. Koda went limp in my arms, her ass tried to tap out after the first round the first night we fucked too. I was going to let her get away with it tonight, but then she uttered those magical words. "I love you, Jax," springing my dick back to life.

Flipping Koda over, I allowed her to be lazy on her back while I slowly dipped inside, stretching her out again. "Say that shit while you cumming on my dick next time," I commanded as she placed her hands on my shoulders and started fucking me back. If the motivational speech Koda gave me earlier didn't cancel my plans of returning to Birmingham, this pussy definitely did.

KODA

A soft nudge to my shoulder prompted my eyes to flutter open. Electricity shot through my body when Jax's sexy ass came into my peripheral. Wearing only a pair of boxer briefs, he would've been enticing but my yoni was sore from the way he wore me out last night.

"Come on bae so you can eat before your interview."

His words jolted me out of bed as I remembered my interview for the part-time job as a CPA. "What time is it?" I questioned, gently rubbing my eyes.

"It's nine o'clock, you got time," Jax assured me, pulling me to my feet.

I went into the bathroom to complete my morning routine before joining Jax in the dining room. Every moment spent with him made me question how I had been missing out on this for all these years. There was a bouquet of bright red roses positioned next to my plate of breakfast food. Collecting them from the table, I hugged them before turning to kiss Jax. I spent years catering to a man who didn't appreciate me, and now I realized that love was a two way street, and Jax poured into me unapologetically.

We ate breakfast, I got dressed in a cute black pants suit and Jax walked me to my new Benz. "You all nervous and shit, let me drive you," Jax offered, opening the door to my car.

"No Jax, I'm a big girl, I'm okay," I declined.

"Never gone be too big for me to be by your side though," Jax replied, pulling me closer to him. He cupped my ass in his big hands and pulled me in for a kiss. I couldn't get enough of the love he gave me. Pulling away from his embrace, I blushed, displaying all of my teeth. "I gotta go before you make me late."

"Alright, I'll be here when you get back," he explained as I climbed into the car. Pulling off, I noticed Jax watching me drive away in my rear view mirror and that made me smile so damn big.

Thirty minutes later I was seated in Tailored Bookkeeping & Tax Services. I did my research on the company last night and was pleasantly surprised to learn that the company was black owned. With the cash Jax pulled out of the crawl space back at my house and the money I put away, I wasn't hurting for money but being home all day was boring. Now that me and Jax were official, the only thing that would come from us sitting at home all day was a baby, and I still had goals I wanted to reach before becoming a mother. Now that I was starting from scratch, a baby was nowhere in my plans.

"Koda?" A beautiful dark skinned woman dressed in a lilac blazer and knee length skirt questioned, entering the lobby.

"Yes," I confirmed, standing with a smile on my face as we shook hands.

"Hello, I'm Dajana, it's nice to meet you."

"Likewise."

"Follow me," she waved me in her direction.

Trailing behind Dajana, I fidgeted with my fingers trying to get my nerves under control. This was my first interview in life. I didn't work as a teenager and Maleek covered my expenses throughout college. When I graduated, Maleek immediately invested in Stellar Financial Services where I started off doing taxes. This was a completely new experience for me and I was determined to nail it.

Dajana pushed a sleek office door open, revealing a sophisticated yet welcoming space. The gold placard on her desk read *Dajana Francis, Owner* and I immediately took notice of the beautiful family pictures placed throughout her office. "Have a seat," she gestured towards the empty chairs opposite of hers.

The scent of freshly brewed coffee lingered in the air as I settled into the plush chair, nerves coiling beneath my confident exterior. Dajana fixed her gaze on me, her expression open and inquisitive. "Relax Koda, would you like a cup of coffee?" She offered.

"No thank you," I declined because that probably would've just messed up my stomach that was already in knots. Plus, Jax stuffed me with pancakes and strawberries before I left the house this morning.

"Okay, well let's dive into your experience," she started and I extended my résumé in her direction.

"Your résumé caught my eye; tell me about your time as the owner of Stellar Financial Services."

I leaned forward, ready to delve into my past. "Running my own financial firm was both challenging and rewarding. Specializing in tax strategies allowed me to develop a keen eye for maximizing returns and minimizing liabilities for clients. I believe my experience has given me a comprehensive understanding of the intricacies of financial management from top to bottom."

Dajana nodded, her interest piqued. "Impressive. Now, considering the shifts in tax regulations, how do you stay updated and ensure compliance for your clients?"

I confidently met her gaze. "The key to success in our field is continuous professional development. I make it a priority to engage in online forums, participate in seminars, and maintain memberships with industry associations. This ensures I'm well-versed in the latest tax codes and can provide the most accurate advice to my clients."

She offered a nod of approval, moving on to more technical questions. "How do you approach financial audits, and can you share an instance where your attention to detail made a significant difference for a client?"

In an affirmative tone, I smiled and answered the question, realizing that this was my bag. I loved this shit and there wasn't a question that Dajana could throw my way that I couldn't answer. "In a previous audit with a new client, my meticulous examination of financial records revealed a discrepancy that was overlooked by their previous CPA. By identifying and rectifying the error, we not only avoided potential legal issues but also secured additional deductions for the client. When it comes to audits, I'm committed to maintaining a high level of precision."

As the interview progressed, Dajana's questions delved into my leadership style, adaptability, and problem-solving abilities. I easily responded with real-life examples, and I could tell she was impressed. Placing the résumé on her desk, Dajana leaned back in her chair before her next question.

"You've said all the right things today, I have to ask why would you want to close your business and work for another firm part-time? Even if you closed your business and relocated I'm sure you had enough clients willing to keep you on remotely.

My smile wavered because I hadn't planned for that question and now I wasn't sure if I should answer honestly or attempt to sugarcoat it. Swallowing hard, I rubbed my thumbs across the palms of my hands before responding.

"I made the mistake of allowing my ex-boyfriend to invest in my business and when things went bad it was best to walk away from the toxicity in all aspects of life. I'm prepared to embark on a fresh start, and I believe this company would be the ideal place to make that happen."

Dajana was visibly satisfied as she stood and leaned over the desk with her hand extended in my direction. "Welcome to the team, Koda. When can you start?"

Gratitude washed over me as I shook her hand. "As soon as you need," I bubbled.

"Let's shoot for Monday and when you come back, save the code switching for the clients, not me and the team. This is a family."

"Thank you so much," I spluttered, fighting off my tears as I was excited about embarking on this new chapter in my life.

Leaving the interview, I felt like I could take on the fucking world. This new start was everything, the only drawback was missing my best friend. I hadn't called her because I knew Simone was the first person that Maleek would question about my whereabouts. Using muscle memory, I dialed her number and prayed that she was on her lunch break.

"Hello," her angelic voice greeted me.

"Simone!" I squealed.

"Kodaaaaaa! Bestie, I miss you so fucking much."

"I miss you too," I chirped.

"I do too but don't bring your ass back here. Maleek really lost his fucking mind. Would you believe he brought his ass over here, kicked Georgie so hard that he fractured a rib, and pulled me by my hair. I don't know what else he would've done if he wouldn't have been down bad from that ass whooping the police put on him."

"Are you serious?" I faltered.

"Dead serious, I had to mace him and run out of the house. He fucked up though because Randal been looking all over for his ass and he ain't nowhere to be found. I also called the police so I could press charges. His stupid ass is in 4K with it. He better hope the police find him before Randal does," she ranted, referring to her older brother that Maleek came up with. Now Randal was the plug for the entire state of Alabama and Maleek was one of his clients.

"I'm so sorry," I lamented, hating that I put her in harm's way. Simone was nothing short of an amazing best friend. She never judged me, was always prepared to lend a listening ear and had my back through everything.

"Don't apologize, that's all on him and he's going to get what the fuck he deserves. He might've got off on whatever charges they were trying to pin on him before but these assault charges are going to stick. He probably won't do no real time but still, he needs to see that he isn't untouchable. Enough about that nigga though, how have you been?"

"Ah-ma-zing," I exulted dramatically.

"Well tell me everything because that was that I got some new dick, amazing."

"I did but promise not to judge me," I shrieked.

"I won't, as long as it's not Maleek," she huffed.

"Not at all," I vehemently denied. "Apparently Maleek was planning to snitch on Jax and he found out so he came and got me before he left Birmingham."

"You fucked Jax!!!" Simone exclaimed.

"Yes I did, and bitch why you ain't tell me that niggas was out here nutting and getting hard right after?! I've been getting mediocre dick all of my life."

Simone scream-laughed and I missed this shit so much. "Bitch, I told you to stop settling for his ass when you told me you be faking orgasms on the regular."

"And I haven't faked one yet with Jax either," I exhaled.

"Oh my God, you all dick whipped and shit. Who would've thought that it would've been by Jax, a nigga who been around since we were kids."

"I know right. Everything is so different with Jax. He matches my energy and I love him," I confessed.

"Girl, you love that dick," Simone retorted.

"No, I love him for real. He's been there for me through some shit and I just love him," I professed.

"If you happy, then I'm happy, Koda. Where are you? How long do I have to wait to come see you? I need a vacation anyways."

"I promised my mom I wouldn't tell anyone where I am. Jax said he don't give a fuck, he was never hiding from Maleek, he was ducking the police. But I'd rather avoid the drama than bring a war to my front door."

"I don't like it, but I get it," she sighed. "If Randal finds Maleek, then you know the first thing I'mma do is hop on a plane to come see you and celebrate."

"Absolutely. Just give me a lil time to ease my mom's concerns and we will plan that trip."

"Okay girl, my lunch break is up and I'm in the parking lot bumping my gums. Let me get in here before they notice I'm gone. I love you and be safe."

"I love you too, talk to you soon."

We ended the call and my spirits were through the roof. I needed that phone call, I had to have that moment with my best friend. As I pulled into the driveway, I noticed that Jax had gone somewhere while I was away; the Honda was now on the right side, unlike a few hours ago when it was on the left. Exiting my car, I barely got out good before Jax opened the front door.

"Damn beautiful, you didn't see a nigga text?" He questioned, exiting the house.

"I forgot to take my phone off vibrate," I replied.

"I just wanted to see if you got hired on the spot. I know you nice like that," Jax suggested.

"I did!" I celebrated, bouncing into his arms.

"Congratulations bae! I knew you was walking out with that shit," he placed his arm around my back, and stared down at me all dreamy and shit. "You motivating a nigga in ways I didn't even know possible."

"You did the same for me, little do you know," I replied.

Jax scooped me off my feet and carried me into the house. I kissed him passionately before he placed me on my feet. Sitting through that interview had me nervous as hell and I was parched. Making a beeline for the kitchen, I grabbed a bottle of water while Jax went into the second bedroom that we never used. When he returned a few moments later with a handful of congratulation balloons, my heart fluttered because Jax was always thinking of ways to put a smile on my face.

"I'm so proud of you bae. Ain't shit you can't do."

"Thank you," I grinned, taking the balloons and planting a kiss on his lips.

He picked me up again, while deepening the kiss. I wrapped my legs around his waist and released my grip on the balloons. "I'mma give you a lil celebratory dick, we gone take a nap, then we are going to meet your parents for dinner to celebrate," Jax announced, carrying me towards the bedroom.

Smiling down at Jax, I didn't have a complaint. The way he treated me and my parents would always solidify Jax's place in my heart.

KODA

"Alright y'all, it's Valentine's Day and my husband has plans for us, so this paperwork can wait until tomorrow. We're wrapping up early today, unless there are any crucial tasks that need attention," Dajana announced at the end of our weekly team lunch.

Every Wednesday Dajana had lunch catered and when she said don't code switch with her, she meant just that. I loved it because it reminded me of my team back in Birmingham so bad. We were professional in front of our clients, but behind closed doors you were liable to catch us making TikTok videos or gossiping about the latest celebrity drama.

"I don't have anything to do." I was the first to explain because Jax had something planned, I just didn't know what it was yet. As a part-time employee, I worked eight hour shifts Monday, Wednesday, and Friday. Since I had to work today Jax requested that I pack an overnight bag last night. I was off tomorrow so I was excited to find out what my man had in store for us tonight.

The buzzer for the front door went off and Dajana quickly glanced at the MacBook in front of her to check the security camera. "It's another flower delivery, whose man came through right before we close up?" She bubbled, hopping from her seat before going to get the door.

She disappeared for a few minutes while the rest of the team packed up their belongings and cleaned the office.

"This is for Koda," Dajana announced, entering the office with an oversized bouquet of pink roses.

Jax already surprised me with two pairs of Balenciaga sneakers this morning, so I wasn't expecting flowers. With a bright smile on my face I accepted the flowers. On my drive home I called Jax and knew he was smoking from the deep exhale he emitted.

"Wassup beautiful?"

"On my way home. Thank you for the flowers," I blushed.

"That's light work. Why you on your way home already?"

"Dajana decided to close the office early for Valentine's Day," I advised him.

"For real?" Jax questioned.

"Yep."

"Alright, I'mma see you when you get home. I had to cancel part of my plans since you had to work today, let me see if I can set it up."

"Alright, see you soon."

We ended the call and I felt like I was floating on cloud nine on my ride home. Being loved correctly was good for the soul. Jax respected my likes and continued to cater to them, showing me that I mattered every step of the way.

When I got home, Jax was dressed in a pair of monogrammed Fendi shorts and there was a matching pair of leggings laid out on the bed for me. If bae wanted to be corny and match for Valentine's Day, I was down. Within two hours I showered, changed, pulled my knotless braids up into a ponytail, and we were on the road. The entire drive over I was wondering what the hell Jax had up his sleeve, the only thing he told me was that we were going to Orlando. The traffic going into Orlando was terrible and I was so happy when Jax got off the interstate. Jax parked in front of a building and I instantly got excited as I looked over at him.

"A helicopter tour, how romantic," I cooed.

"I'm trying to do what I gotta do to keep you smiling like that," he expressed.

We entered the building and Jax checked in while I scanned the snack selection. Settling on the drumstick ice cream cone to help me occupy my time until it was our turn. The sun was starting to set by the time it was our time for our tour. Jax helped me into the helicopter, and we snuggled up while we ascended in the air. I have been on airplanes, but this was my first time in a helicopter, so I was slightly nervous.

"This ride is slightly symbolic for us, the sky is the limit baby." Jax interrupted the silence as I recorded videos from our position.

"And our love is soaring to new heights... my shit was corny, I know," I chuckled, and Jax joined in with a laugh.

The helicopter soared above fascinating landscapes, and I couldn't help but feel a rush of excitement coursing through me. This was an experience I didn't even know I needed. Rhythmic thumping of the blades and the panoramic view below created a surreal experience, made even more special by the hand I held tightly—Jax, his eyes reflecting the adoration mirrored in my own. Laying my head on his shoulder, I couldn't imagine my life without this man, it wouldn't be worth living.

JAX

Koda's reaction to the helicopter tour was worth the hours I spent online searching for something romantic to do for Valentine's Day. I never had a girlfriend and all of this shit was new to me, but it came easy because I was doing it for Koda, the woman whose energy I craved. The intense and sudden attachment I had to Koda was weird as fuck at first, and I didn't want to succumb to it. Especially after learning that I could return to Birmingham without consequences from the law. We were a few weeks into this journey and I didn't want it to end.

After the helicopter tour, we had to drive fifteen minutes north to Norman's Orlando for our dinner reservations. When we entered the restaurant, the shit was as nice as Mrs. Allen described. Guiding Koda to our table, I felt her hand tighten around mine when she spotted her parents already seated, sipping on cocktails while they waited for us.

"You brought my parents?" Koda questioned.

"Yeah, your mama said I been hogging you to myself since you started working so I told them to join us tonight."

Koda bounced over to her parents, enveloping them in warm hugs, and as they exchanged greetings, I pulled out her chair for her to take a seat. As the warmth of family surrounded us, Koda's smile lit up the room. Mr. and Mrs. Allen welcomed me with open arms since we got to Florida. I halfway didn't think they would remember me from all of those years ago, I always felt like a forgotten child, but Koda's parents showed me that wasn't the case.

"So now that it's clear y'all are together when are you going to find a permanent home? I know you're wasting money with that Airbnb." Mrs. Allen pried over dessert.

"We are going to start looking when we get back. I just wanted to make sure that we find a spot that's not too far from my job, and also not too far from you guys," Koda replied.

"You sure y'all aren't moving too fast?" Mr. Allen tossed out there, looking between me and Koda. This was her family and I was taking the backseat. I also wanted to hear Koda's answer because she was fresh out of a relationship, just had an abortion, and I didn't want to put anything on her that she couldn't handle.

"I'm sure daddy. Never been more sure about anything else in my life," Koda smiled, placing her hand on top of mine.

"Well what you got going on for work, Jax? I ain't heard a word about that."

"I'm sitting on some money. I can hold my own while I figure out my next move. Don't get it twisted though, Koda don't pay for nothing while I'm around, really don't know why she went back to work but that was her choice."

"Go 'head and get him together, Jax," Mrs. Allen sipped her water.

"Stop ma, we don't have anything to hide. Dad can ask as many questions as he needs to feel comfortable," Koda assured them.

The waitress returned with the check and I passed her my credit card. One thing I ain't never had to worry about was money. Koda didn't either. Leaving the steakhouse we got in our cars and Mr. Allen trailed me to the last stop of the night, The Wine Room. Entering the establishment Koda and Mrs. Allen were excited as hell. I paid for everyone's cards and they perused the wine selection tasting various wines without a care in the world. Although me and Mr. Allen weren't into wine, we had a card. I was about to indulge since there wasn't shit else to do, but Mr. Allen pulled me away from the women and slipped a small silver flask into my hand.

"Ain't nobody about to be drinking this shit. I brought some Hennessy for us," he explained. Laughing, I accepted the flask and took a small swig of the liquor with Mr. Allen. "Look, I won't say too much, just treat Koda right. I saw how hard she was smiling at you all night, and I can see that you care about her too. At the same time, it does scare me that Koda barely left Maleek before y'all started whatever this is..."

"Ion mean to cut you off but this is some real shit, I ain't coming up off of Koda. I get that y'all been through some things with Koda and her last nigga but that ain't me. Now I won't stand here and act like a perfect stand up nigga, Koda is the first real relationship I ever been in but I assure you it's my last."

"Trust me, if I even suspect that you are anything like that last nigga..." Mr. Allen seethed before his voice trailed off and it was like he disappeared for a minute. "If I thought you were anything like that nigga, I would've shot you on my doorstep. Never letting my daughter get sucked up with a nigga like that again. Just wish she would've taken some time for herself instead of jumping head first into a new relationship so soon."

"I get it, I do but Koda is in good hands. The threats you throw out there probably blank, but when I say I'll lay a nigga down behind your daughter, I mean that."

"Oh my threats aren't empty," he laughed.

"Man, Mr. Allen, you probably don't even own a gun," I joked.

"I had no choice but to get one after my last run in with Maleek."

"You had a run in with Maleek?"

"Yeah, it was about a year ago. Just don't tell Koda."

"Well what happened?" I questioned.

"Give me your word."

"You got my word, I won't say shit."

Mr. Allen took another swig from his flask then looked around to confirm the women's location. "They straight over there sipping their second glass while looking for their third. I haven't lost sight of them since we walked over here," I nodded in their direction.

"I didn't hurt myself on the job like we told Koda. About two years ago we had a big blow up. Koda confessed to her mother that Maleek put his hands on her and when I talked to her I told her to leave. She wouldn't, so we caught a flight up there and tried to get her to come home with us. Me and Maleek got to tussling when he came home. I wanted to kill that nigga after I saw the marks on Koda's arms. At the end of it all, Koda decided to stay and my wife forced me to leave. After that, Koda changed her number and we couldn't get in touch with her. We popped up at their house again after about a year and found out they moved. Simone told us she couldn't get in the middle and that Koda was alright, but didn't want to be bothered so we knew she was straight, but I still wanted to lay eyes on my daughter so I hired a private investigator to find Koda or Maleek. I guess the PI's in the area are in Maleek's pocket because they told him we were looking for him after taking my money. He brought his ass to Atlanta and caught me off guard. When I was coming out of work he walked up on me and said some shit like he heard I was looking for him so, I caught him in the jaw. Got the best of that nigga so he decided to shoot me in the leg."

"Nah man, say you swear?"

"Put that on my daughter," he confirmed, eyeing the women across the way. "After that, Cali told me to leave Koda be. Said when she was ready to come home, she would. I don't always listen to my wife but when I do, her ass be right every time."

KODA

Seated at my desk in the compact office space assigned to me, I couldn't deny the significant shift from being a business owner to now working as an employee. The shit was freeing. When I left the office, work was over. I didn't have to handle my clients and help my employees so I was loving this change. Of course I still planned to work for myself in the future, but this was perfect for now.

My desk showcased a picture of me, Jax, and my parents from Valentine's Day at The Wine Room and a bright smile spread across my face every time I caught a glimpse of it. Focusing on the self-employed tax return in front of me, I double checked the information one final time before calling the client to discuss their tax bill for the year. After ending the call, I checked my phone and saw Jax text me that he was pulling up. At least once a week Jax came to have lunch with me and I was bouncing in my seat because he drove all the way to Tampa this morning to get food from a Jamaican restaurant. I went to let Jax in and led him directly to my office because I was hungry as fuck. He closed the door behind him and took a seat while I grabbed some hand sanitizing wipes for us. Opening the to-go carton, I worked on the rice and peas first. Halfway through with my food I was stuffed and closing the container.

"Yo ass didn't eat that food this morning did you?" Jax questioned, closing his carton.

"I didn't," I chuckled. "As soon as I got here, I had to hit the ground running and I forgot."

"You need to start waking up earlier so you can eat before you leave then."

"I'm not going to starve to death Jax," I retorted. "Ion know what you like doing more, fucking or feeding me."

"Definitely fucking you," he grinned, leaning back in his chair.

"If only I wasn't at work," I bit my bottom lip.

"Shit, we can lock the door and I can cover yo loud mouth," he suggested, and I could see in his eyes that he meant it.

"Boy, no. I did get you something though," I bubbled, rummaging through my desk.

"What is it?"

Pulling a brand new MacBook out of my drawer, I placed the box on the desk for Jax to see.

"You ain't have to spend your money on that, Koda."

"I didn't, but I wanted to. You're always buying me nice things and I wanted to do it for you," I explained, walking to his side of the desk.

"Well I appreciate it," Jax accepted the box and pulled me down in his lap. His free hand found their way to the hem of my pencil skirt and my silly ass wasn't about to fight him either. He smelled so fucking good like always and I planted a kiss on his neck.

KNOCK! KNOCK! KNOCK!

I hopped off of his lap and pulled my skirt back down before rounding my desk. "You can come in."

Dajana entered my office, her face buried in the file gripped tightly in her hand. "Would you mind..." Her voice trailed off when she almost tripped over Jax's foot.

"Oh excuse me, I didn't know your lunch date was here. I don't know who is up here more, Jax or my husband," she laughed. "How are you today, Jax?"

"Straight," he nodded.

"Good, I'm sorry to interrupt but I have another client for you to follow up with. He is usually one of my clients, but I warned him that you would get him squared away for today."

"You know I got you," I bubbled, accepting the file from her.

She left as swiftly as she came and I chuckled at the thought of almost getting caught.

"I appreciate you for real, Koda. It's been forever since a nigga was showed love like this."

"You're welcome, I figured it could help you along the way in whatever you decide to do."

"I almost forgot. I actually did a lil questionnaire this morning and printed out the results. It gave me a handful of jobs I might be good at based on my answers," Jax explained, pulling a folded up piece of paper out of his pocket.

I retrieved it from his hand, took a moment to read through it, and then offered my opinion. "We can cross martial arts instructor off because you don't like people like that. Private investigators have to keep late hours and I like you home in the bed with me at night, so that won't work either," I paused and tapped my chin with the tips of my index and middle finger. "Would you really want to be somebody's bodyguard?"

"Fuck no," Jax shook his head and I crossed it off the list.

"That leaves you with a cybersecurity expert. It says you will protect digital assets and information. You're good on a computer right?" I questioned, opening my MacBook.

"Stop playing with me," Jax shrugged.

"I'm just asking because I've never seen you use any electronics other than your phone," I joked.

"That's because I haven't needed to. I know my way around a computer though," he confirmed as I did a quick google search.

"Well it looks like USF and UCF offer a six month online course where you can earn your certificate. Ohhhhh and there is a black owned cyber security company that's felon friendly in Tampa."

"What you trying to say?" Jax laughed.

"Nothing, it's just a good sign that the owners will be down to earth and not them uppity niggas. Oh and it says he offers mentorship for those looking to start their own companies," I bubbled. "I think this is the one, what do you think?"

"I think it's beautiful how much you believe in me," Jax commented, leaning over the desk to kiss my lips before standing. "That's actually the only one that caught my eye. I'mma look into the program and see what else I can learn about the field once I get home."

"Taking initiative is so sexy on you."

"Ain't never been one to sit on my ass looking clueless," he clarified. "I'm telling you now though, you rushed to get back to work but this time next year, you'll have your own shit."

"Absolutely," I affirmed, standing to walk him out.

After Jax left I finished up the rest of my work and went to the spa my mom worked at part time. Jax booked a massage and I needed it badly. The spa was so cute and my mom came out and greeted me in her scrubs, looking all professional and shit before leading me to a room and instructing me to strip down. The combination of soft soothing music and lavender scent wafting through the dimly lit room, instantly eased the tension from my shoulders as I settled onto the plush massage table.

My mom knocked and entered the room getting down to business. I was pleasantly surprised as her skilled hands began to work their magic, kneading away the knots and stress accumulated from the demands of life.

"I love Jax for you. Our Valentine's Day getaway was perfect. It took everything out of me not to get emotional because I never thought I'd get to experience those moments. Spending time with your person and we actually like... no, love him."

"I was shocked to see you guys seated at the table. I just knew we were about to have a nice dinner alone. The helicopter ride would have sufficed but he really went above and beyond for me. I've never experienced the type of treatment that Jax gives me."

"Well you know your dad is still weary, I think he'll be like that for a while," she detailed, applying rhythmic pressure to my shoulders. Her skilled hands made this uncomfortable conversation easier.

"I know that I put you guys through a lot and I apologize again."

"You don't have to keep apologizing. Life is all about lessons and I hope that you learned them. It does make me nervous that you are quickly falling into things with Jax, but I'm not fearful. He includes us in things, doesn't mind coming over and your smile is genuine. I can feel it."

"Yeah, I love him and it scared me at first but I can't help it, ma." I expressed as my muscles untangled and tension dissipated.

"No matter what though, make sure you love yourself first," she paused and I turned my head to the side to see what she was doing. My mom leaned down and kissed my cheek.

"I'll never let that happen again," I allowed a few tears to roll down my face as I repositioned my head into the massage table. The remainder of our time was silent. As the session neared its end, I knew that the massage had not only rejuvenated my body, but had also granted a reprieve to my mind.

MALEEK

Taking a swig straight from the bottle of Hennessy, I tossed that bitch across the room when I realized that there wasn't shit else in this file cabinet to look through. Day forty-two of life without Koda and it was beating my ass. She cooked, cleaned, and made sure a nigga's head was on straight. I didn't realize how much I needed Koda until she was gone. After going through every file I removed from Koda's office, I didn't find shit to lead me back to her. I lost optimism a while back, Koda was an expert at hiding money, and I had to see this shit through. After having a forensic accountant look into our accounts, I discovered the bitch was slowly moving small amounts of money out of our business accounts once a month to an account in her own name. My life was spiraling out of control and I knew it.

Now I was living off of Hennessy and takeout while in hiding. When I got to Simone's house I never planned to approach her in the manner in which I did, but one thing led to another and I snapped. Now I had to worry about her brother Randal on my ass. Growing up it was me, Randal and Kenneth, running the streets, getting into a bunch of shit that we had no business in.

Randal came from a white pickett fence family but he was a wild ass nigga, had been since we were young. He jumped off the porch first, knee deep in the trenches, slanging dope for Jordans and shit. Then when Kenneth and Jax's mom was murdered and their father was sent to prison for life, me and Kenneth joined him. My parents provided for all of my wants and most of my needs, I decided to get in the streets because my niggas were in the streets. Looking back, I acknowledge that I was on some follow the leader ass shit. It's funny because Randal's and my parents thought that Kenneth was the ring-leader, and that was the furthest from the truth. If it wasn't for his circumstances, Kenneth would've kept his warehouse job and worked his way through college. Unfortunately, life didn't work that way.

Fast forward over a decade and Kenneth was dead, I had Birmingham on lock and Randal was the plug for the entire state of Alabama. After my actions with Simone, the partnership between me and Randal was dead. Word on the streets, the nigga wanted my head so I was ducked off somewhere that Randal would never think to look for me. I fucked up and now I was reduced to this lil apartment in country ass Bessmer while I figured my shit out. With every passing day, my chances of rebuilding my team and reclaiming my throne seemed increasingly bleak.

On top of me running up in Simone's house. Randal was also pissed that he hadn't received his re-up money that Jax was on his way to deliver before shit went sour. That young nigga was running with my bitch and three million of my hard earned dollars. Since I was all in that nigga's business, I knew he had way more than that put up, so it didn't make any sense to take my shit. Now I was out of three million, I owed the plug money, and I couldn't trust the niggas I had on my team.

All of these thoughts swirling around in my head had a nigga craving a drink, my life was falling apart and I didn't have a solid plan to stop it. As bad as the craving was, I just fed the last of the Hennessy to the wall. Snatching my keys off the counter, I headed to the liquor store to grab another bottle.

Pulling up to the liquor store, I sat in Koda's AMG for a moment to check my surroundings. My hope was that driving it would make it harder for Randal or his people to spot me, than if I was driving one of my own whips. Once I felt secure, I stepped out the car and a young nigga peddling fast as fuck on a BMX bike rolled up on me. I gripped my gun, ready to send his young ass to hell if he was on some funny shit.

"Say mane, can you grab a bottle of Patron for me and my boys? We having a lil kick back, I can pay you..." He paused his statement mid sentence and blinked twice once he scanned my face. "Yooooo, Maleek! OG, we been waiting to hear from you or Jax about what to do, shit fucked up, my people in a drought bad after what happened with Madden. Then you got locked up, Jax went missing, and we been waiting to make a play."

"You used to work with Madden?" I questioned. Jax was supposed to put them niggas down after they stepped over in our territory. Clearly the nigga was going soft. I guess that's why he popped up unannounced at my house that day.

"Yeah, then when he got got, Jax said he was gone put us on if we keep shit quiet and cleaned the mess up," he stated.

"Oh yeah," I nodded, my wheels turning faster than they had in days. This was it, I had an in and it was all due to Jax.

"What's yo name?"

"Speedy," he declared proudly. I examined his clothes and shoes, the lil nigga might not have had dope to sell but he looked decent, he was a hustler.

"You said you need a bottle of Patron, right?" I clarified.

"Grab me three," he stated, dipping his hand in his pocket. I noticed the gun on his waist as he pulled a small knot of hundreds out of his pocket to compensate me for the Patron.

"Nah, I got you," I declined his money. "Wait right here, I'mma grab you this bottle and we gone chop it up."

"Good lookin'," he smiled.

I went into the liquor store, grabbed five bottles of Patron, a bottle of D'Usse and met Speedy back in the parking lot. "Come take a ride with me," I commanded.

"But my bike," he noted.

"Fuck that bike, we'll get you some wheels," I assured him.

"Ion have no license."

"Damn, you gotta at least be eighteen, your people ain't taught you to drive yet?" I questioned, to check his age without being overt with my questioning.

"Nah, my mama don't have a car so she ain't taught me yet. I'm seventeen, I have my learners permit, so as soon as I get my bread up I'll get a car, then I'll learn to drive."

"Well, I'll get you another bike,we got business to handle," I explained. Speedy didn't know it, but he was going to be my protégé. Just like I taught Jax all he knows, I could do that shit again, ten times over.

Speedy hopped in the passenger seat and I got right down to business as he directed me to the spot his boys were hanging at. "Look, shit fucked up," I started, backing out of the parking spot. "Crackas on a nigga bad so I can't make too many moves out here but if you willing to take the lead while I lay low, I can get shit in motion. There is one condition though."

"What's that?" He inquired, pointing for me to turn left.

"You can't tell a motha fuckin' soul that I'm fronting you the money. You can be my right hand because Jax stepped out of the game and..."

"For real?" He questioned eagerly. Yeah, the lil nigga was built for this shit, I can feel it just like I did with Jax. "For real, I'll get your mama a whip, put her up in a crib and make sure y'all straight. Who else knows about what happened to Madden?"

"Shit, nobody but us," he shrugged. "It was like six of us out there that night and Jax told us to get rid of the body and we did. Madden only had his baby mamas but they was always beefing, he owed them hella child support, they just think the nigga trying to get away from his responsibilities."

"That's what's up. You ever heard of Randal Mitchelle out of Huntsville?"

"Everybody know he the plug."

"He might be nervous to fuck with you because you young as fuck, so who you got on your team that's a lil older that you would trust with some shit like this?"

"My older brother, Marlo. He just got out a few days before the shit happened with Madden."

"Alright, I gotta meet him before I give you the play. Need to feel that nigga out, see if I can trust him, if I can, we in business."

"Bet, pull up to that beige house on the corner," Speedy directed.

I pulled up to the curb and there was a group of about seven or eight young niggas, shirts off, hands gripping their waist, ready to shoot this shit up if we didn't announce ourselves. Speedy let his window down and they all relax. I saw enough, this was exactly what I needed. Pausing for a moment, I looked up at the sky and thanked the lord for coming through in the clutch. With this crew of young hungry niggas, I'd be back on top in no time.

"So let me ask you this, y'all got any real hittas on your team? I'm talking not scared to push a niggas mama shit back if it comes to that?"

"Definitely Marlo," he pointed to the one I noticed earlier because he was still on high alert even after seeing Speedy in my passenger seat. A light skinned nigga with a mouth full of gold teeth and a pair of menacing eyes, reminded me of a young hood version of Jax.

"Talk to yo brother, get your crew in order and hit me when you ready to get down," I explained, scribbling my number on the back of a business card sitting in the cupholder.

"Bet."

KODA

"Where is dad?" I asked my mom as she slid into the backseat of my Benz.

"He went somewhere with our neighbor Robert. He is always hanging with the men in our neighborhood and I don't care as long as they keep their talking ass wives away from my house. I tried to be social like Kyle but no thanks, they came over while they went fishing and spent our time crying about what their husbands don't do. Sorry boo, I can't relate, Kyle would've been left in the dust if he was a bum."

"Ma," I snickered as Jax shook his head, backing out of her driveway.

"I'm for real, they think I wanna be social because Kyle is always taking his ass somewhere with their husbands. The desperate housewives are partly why I got a part-time job. I didn't want to turn into them and it helped me stop them from coming to my house inviting me to shit that I always had to decline. I enjoy my own company. Plus the ladies from the spa invite me out every now and again. That's enough for me. Hopefully y'all will give me some grandbabies soon."

"No time soon," I refuted. "I'm living it up in my twenties and building the foundation to have kids in my thirties. Jax is twenty-four, and I'm twenty-six, we have plenty of time. Our relationship is fresh and we'll cross that bridge in another five or six years. I at least need a ring first."

"A ring ain't shit, we can get married tomorrow if you want to," Jax lifted my hand to his lips and kissed the knuckle.

"Boy, that's not how you ask," I rolled my eyes.

"I wasn't asking, just wondering. When I'm asking you gone know, I ain't half stepped yet have I?"

"Not at all," I bubbled.

Jax was driving and I was riding shotgun. As we officially embraced Florida as our forever home, it was time to move out of the Airbnb and into our own place. After asking Jax how much he paid a night, my mother was right, he was burning through money. I know that it didn't bother Jax, he had money to blow and wasn't in a rush to do anything. A part of me felt like Jax was dragging his feet about the matter because Birmingham was still calling him. I knew it would be hard for him to leave the streets alone; eight years, that shit was in his blood. My palms got sweaty just thinking about this shit because a part of me didn't feel like my love would be enough to keep Jax on this path.

His hand landed on my thigh, jolting me from my overwhelming thoughts. It was then that I noticed I had nervously started peeling the skin off my bottom lip. "You straight?"

"Yeah," I lied, offering the fakest smile I could muster. "Lil nervous about telling ma our plan."

"And what's that?" She interjected just as I expected.

"We want to move to Tampa. I'm working remotely two out of the three days now, so commuting won't be an issue. Plus, it's bigger, offers more opportunities, and it's still not too far from you guys. A quick forty or fifty minute drive is nothing compared to the distance that previously separated us."

"Come on y'all, what happened to wanting to find a place close to us and your job?" she whined. I turned to face her in the backseat and her lip was poked out with her arms folded across her chest. "Jax, why would you bring our baby home just to take her away from us again?" She glared at the back of his head, wearing a contemptuous expression.

"I promise it's not like that, Mrs. Allen," Jax argued. "I was cool living in Clearwater, that's Koda wanna move to Tampa."

"Ahhhh," she clutched her chest, crumpling her lavender shirt with her mouth agape. "Koda, is this true?"

"Girllll," I giggled, spinning back around. "Please stop being dramatic back there."

"If y'all want, we can move y'all to the city too," Jax offered.

"No, I love my job, house, and neighborhood."

"Ma, you was just talking about how the desperate housewives get on your nerves. You can't like the neighborhood too much."

"I don't like the wives, that's completely different from the neighborhood. It's quiet, I just got used to knowing my way around there."

"It's only been what, three months?"

"More like five or six now, but who is counting. Y'all just gone have to make the drive to come see us just as often as you do now."

We talked mess the duration of the forty minute drive to downtown Tampa. Jax parked on the street and I was observing everything from the traffic, to parking, and the nearby restaurants. If we chose this condo, this would be my first time living downtown and so far, I wasn't convinced. The traffic was atrocious, horns blaring all over, and pedestrians seemed to be everywhere. I was used to my quiet jogs and visits to the botanical gardens – this bustling scene wasn't appealing at all. Everything was moving entirely too fast. However, Jax swore he loved living downtown in Birmingham so I was going to entertain the idea.

"I thought y'all said we were going to look at a new place for y'all? Why are we here?" My mom quizzed.

"We are, the same realtor that helped Koda find your house is about to show us a few properties today. First is the one at the top of my list, a two bedroom condo on the eleventh floor with a view," Jax was trying to sell both of us on this idea because I'm sure he noticed my apprehensive demeanor.

"Y'all need to think big. I know Koda is going to want to turn that second bedroom into an office so where will I sleep when I come over."

"You won't, you'll go home," I laughed.

"Wowwwww, but I always opened my doors for you though," she put on the dramatics again as we exited the car.

Interlocking my arm into my mother's, I snuggled up against her shoulder and we rounded the corner, approaching the entrance with Jax on our heels. Upon entering we were immediately greeted by Tessa, the realtor that helped us swiftly find my parents home. Once we were inside of the building it was quiet, slow, and I felt slightly at ease.

"Hello, nice to see you again Mrs. Allen," Tessa greeted my mother before turning to us. "You must be Jax and Koda, nice to meet you guys."

We exchanged pleasantries and she led us throughout the building, showcasing the various amenities. Tessa clarified that there was around-the-clock security, and only occupants, and security personnel were authorized to buzz people in. Additionally, the elevators required a fob for operation. The security measures reassured me, making me reconsider the condo lifestyle already. Tessa then took a moment to guide us through the amenities – the two gyms, the community center featuring a movie theater, pool hall, and several pools and hot tubs all stood out as impressive features.

However, when we entered the unit that was available for sale, I was floored. The kitchen was smaller than I was used to coming from my old home, but Jax did most of the cooking these days anyways. Once I saw the floor to ceiling windows throughout the condo that showcased downtown, I was sold.

"You like this shit don't you?" Jaxed questioned, easing up on me from behind. His hard chest collided with my back and his arms slid around my waist. I paused to savor the moment, envisioning us in the same spot, soaking in the view after a long day of work. The thoughts of a future with Jax brought a smile to my face, and I couldn't help but love the idea.

His phone rang and he broke our embrace to take the call in the hallway. My mother exited the room Tessa took her in and came back over with a smile on her face. "I love this for you guys, I wasn't sold. I took Tessa in there to ask her why she was trying to move you guys so far away but I get it. We don't want to smother you but I sure am going to miss you guys being ten minutes away."

"It'll still feel like ten minutes," I assured my mom before hugging her tightly. Over the years, I put my parents through a lot and that would probably haunt me until the end of my days.

"Are you guys ready to see the house in Town and Country?" Tessa inquired, checking the time on her Apple Watch.

"I really don't think we need to see anything else. Jax already had his heart set on this one and now you sold me on it too," I explained.

The door swung open, and Jax sauntered inside. His shift in demeanor was almost hidden, but having spent so much time with Jax, I picked up on the subtle changes. That smile was forced, and his face bore the weight of unspoken turmoil, with worry lines on his forehead standing out to me.

"Before we go see the other houses just remember we can buy this, stay here for a few years while we get our businesses in order then buy a house and rent this out," Jax stated, concealing whatever was plaguing him. He wasn't the type of man to bite his tongue, so I knew this was something we needed to discuss in private.

"No, we don't have to go see those other houses. I just told Tessa that we can put in an offer if you're still sold on it now that you saw it in person."

"I'm with it, put that offer in and get us moved in, Tessa," Jax smiled.

"I'll get on it as soon as I walk you guys out," Tessa bubbled. This unit was on the market for half a million so I'm sure she was excitedly counting her commission. My mother was just happy to be here and I was ready to get home to figure out what was wrong with my man.

The drive back to Clearwater was quiet. My mom fell asleep and Jax maneuvered through traffic with his eyes continuously alternating between the road and his phone.

"Is everything okay?" I finally asked while we drove across the Howard Franklin bridge.

The shit was eating me up inside not knowing what the phone call he took pertained to, and why it upset him. My thoughts went back to my insecurities. Was I enough to keep Jax out of the streets?

"We'll talk about it when we get to the crib."

I didn't like his answer but I understood. Biting my cheek, the drive home couldn't go any faster. With the afternoon traffic, it took an hour to reach my mom's house and it was nearing lunch time.

"I thought we were going to lunch?" She asked after I gently nudged her awake.

"Something came up at work so we will have to do lunch another day."

"Alright baby, let me know when y'all make it home," she requested before exiting the car.

We watched until my dad opened the door and waved at us before backing out of the driveway. Once we were safely inside of our own place, I went to the kitchen to grab the bottle of D'Usse he kept in the kitchen and poured me a shot.

"What the fuck is you doing?" Jax inquired, snatching the glass before I could drink it.

"You about to leave me and go back to Birmingham. I know it, I can see it all over your face so the least you can do is let me drink the pain away."

"Man stop that shit," he urged, setting the glass down and grabbing me by the waist, gently placing me on the counter. Nuzzling his head into the crook of my neck, we lingered in silence for a few moments, and that was all the confirmation I needed. Exhaling deeply, I shoved Jax away, attempting to hop off the counter, but he quickly raised his hands to keep me in position.

"Just say it... just say it! Man the fuck up, Jax and fucking say it!" I shouted, fighting to free myself from his grasp. He wrapped his arms around me like a fucking bear and I stopped squirming because there was no use. "Tell me you wanna move back to Birmingham, I get it, you not ready to leave that life yet."

"Man, fuck is you talkin' 'bout?" Jax wondered, pulling himself away from me and cupping my chin so we were eye to eye. "I'm only going back to Birmingham to handle one business move, get my trucks shipped down here and clean out my old spot. When I took off I left behind a lot of sentimental shit, my mama and brother's ashes, pictures, shit I can't replace. I know you don't want me to go back and shit but Koda, Maleek don't pump no fear in me and honestly, it don't make me feel good that he put that kind of fear in yo heart." He grimaced, releasing my face and placing his hand on my chest. "You went down to working remote two out of three days because of your anxiety, and he plays into that shit."

"But why do you have to go back now all of a sudden? We just put in an offer on the condo. Why can't you wait until we get that situated before you go back home?"

"I gotta go now. When we slid, I left shit in shambles, niggas depend on me and Maleek to feed their families. According to niggas that done laid their life on the line for me, they fucked up and I gotta go make shit right." I rolled my eyes and looked up at the ceiling as he continued. "If I don't go now you'll just keep asking me to push the shit back. I know it's fucked up that I sprung this shit on you but if I would've given you notice you would've pouted just like you are now and probably made me go against everything I stand for."

"So when are you leaving? How long are you going to be gone for?" I quizzed, clearly still frustrated.

"Tonight and I'm coming back to you as soon as shit is handled," Jax confessed. There was no arguing with him, I saw it in his eyes. If it was up to me, Jax would never go back to Birmingham, but that would make life too easy.

I groaned loudly, making my disdain for his decision clear. Then this slick ass nigga leaned in and kissed my neck, and trailed his tongue down the left side before alternating to the right. His hands went between my legs, massaging my pussy through my cotton shorts. I threw my arms across his shoulders and opened my legs to give him easier access. A sense of uncertainty engulfed me, spreading from the crown of my head to the soles of my feet. I pushed that feeling to the side and fumbled with Jax's jeans, there was no need to fight a losing battle, I'd rather enjoy the earth shattering orgasms he always blessed me with and go from there.

Once his dick was free, I slightly lifted up from the counter to help Jax get my shorts and panties off. His middle and index finger found their way to my slit and he slid his fingers inside, driving my craving for him. Placing his thumb on my clit, the pressure felt so good, in a short amount of time he learned my body effortlessly.

"Shit," I hissed, as Jax removed his fingers from my center and sucked my juices off them before leaning in to kiss me. That was one of his favorite things to do and I didn't mind at all.

"I promise I'm coming right back to this," he expressed, leveling his dick with my opening while staring into my eyes.

I nodded my head, biting my bottom lip while placing my hands on his shoulders again. Scooting to the edge of the counter, Jax leaned in and kissed me, while easing his dick into its favorite place. He offered slow strokes, while kissing me and I was savoring every moment of it.

"I love you, Koda," Jax professed.

Before I could reciprocate, he wrapped his arm around my back and pulled me off the counter, bouncing me up and down on his dick. I loved the way he was able to fuck me in various positions, whether he had leverage or not. The slow strokes were over, and my juices were running out of me as he worked my pussy with deep hard thrusts.

"I said, I love you, Koda," he repeated himself.

"I love you too, Jax!" I screamed at the top of my lungs as an orgasm ripped through me.

My body jerked in his arms and Jax smiled, signaling that he wasn't about to let up. Pulling his dick out, it was still long and strong as he spun me around and leaned me over the counter. I wasn't tall enough to touch the ground in this position so I had to hold on to the counter.

"You see how much I love this shit?" Jax questioned, rubbing his dick up and down my slit.

"Yes baby," I cooed, impatiently waiting for what I knew was inevitable.

"You believe me when I say, I love you?" He questioned, planting a kiss on the back of my neck.

"Yes baby."

"Then fucking act like it," he ordered, ramming his dick inside of me while slapping my ass.

"I am!" I cried out, holding onto the counter as he went in and out of me like he had a point to prove.

"No, the fuck you not," Jax stated, pulling me into his chest by my hair. "You acting like you don't believe a nigga coming back."

"I... I do," I stuttered.

Jax gripped my waist and bounced me up and down until I felt that tingly sensation rising.

"Cum all over this dick bae, mark yo shit up before I leave," he commanded, biting on my earlobe and I was spent.

My walls clenched his dick as I gave him my second orgasm. This one was more powerful than the first and I was ready to tap out. Jax pulled his dick out and I dropped to my knees, ready to catch his nut. "Where you want it?"

I flicked out my tongue and he bought his dick closer to my mouth so I could suck him in. Pulling the nut out of him, I offered a bright smile.

"Fuck!" Jax exclaimed, holding the counter for leverage.

I sucked out every drop and swallowed it while he pulled his dick out of my mouth. Standing to my feet, I was tired as a newborn, barely able to keep my eyes open as I was still getting used to having more than one orgasm at a time.

"You tired bae?" Jax asked, pulling me closer to him.

"Yeah," I nodded, rubbing my eyes.

"Come on," he stated, guiding me towards the bedroom by my waist.

As soon as I hit the pillow, I was knocked out. When my eyes fluttered open at nine o'clock, I realized it was all a scheme, as Jax was gone and his phone was laying on the nightstand. Slick ass nigga.

JAX

Koda didn't need to vocalize it; she didn't think I was coming back. Whether she feared I wouldn't make it back or that I'd choose to remain in Birmingham, I meant every word when I vowed to come back to her. I didn't even pack a bag; I didn't plan on staying a minute longer than I had to. Twenty-four hours was my ideal deadline, but we'll see how smooth this shit went. Walking out of Birmingham International Airport, I spotted Corey's F-150 sitting in the pickup lanes.

Yesterday when I stepped out of the condo to take that call, he let me know that some people spotted Maleek in Bessemer and I felt like this was the perfect opportunity to handle him since he was walking around free. He knew too much about me and could sell me out to the Feds at any time, plus I unintentionally took Koda and the quickest way to make a nigga tender is to fuck with his bitch. Above all else, Koda was really fearful of that nigga and I couldn't go for that. My lady was going to walk the streets without looking over her shoulders, biting on her lips and shit. She deserved a soft life after dealing with that fuck nigga for years.

Once I found out Maleek got off on them charges and Koda went back to work, I took a little time to put this plan in motion. The niggas who used to be on my team setup a couple of traps amongst themselves, with Corey at the forefront, moving the drugs they lifted from the warehouse after I left. If they had the connection with the plug they wouldn't need me, I was proud of how well I taught them. Especially when most of them niggas was older than me.

"Wassup," I dapped Corey up once I was seated in the truck.

"Shit, heavy is the head that wears the crown. I got..." he shook his head and I raised my hand for him to shut the fuck up.

I might've had my feet up in Florida for a minute but this shit was in my blood and I didn't talk in cars. Corey nodded his head and we drove in silence until we made it to the spot to meet Randal at. The jogger set Koda bought me a few weeks ago was finally getting some use since the temperatures were in the fifties now that the sunset in Birmingham. Stepping out of the car, the winds slapped me in my face and I missed this shit, Florida was hot as hell. Sometimes I'd forget it wasn't the summer months.

Rounding the truck, we were a few minutes early for our meeting with Randal, and Corey met me in the middle.

"Come on nigga, you know better, never talk that shit in the car. You wearing the crown right?"

"Hell yeah," Corey affirmed.

"Then fucking move like it. You in charge now, niggas depend on you to lead and you gotta lead by example or else get the fuck out the way because that shit there," I pointed to the cabin of his truck before I continued, "makes it too easy for the Feds to listen."

"Understood and it won't happen again."

"Let me stop preaching," I tried to relax. "This yo shit now."

"Nah, you right and I'mma tighten the fuck up."

"Good, Ion wanna see yo face on the news in a few years. You gotta make sure that them niggas under you do the same or else they'll get caught up in some shit and no matter how loyal you think a nigga is, they may fold. Maleek taught me that. Now what were you about to say?"

"Shit, I uhhh, was just was gone say..."

"Stop talkin' like you nervous and shit. Speak with yo chin up and chest out at all times, don't waiver, even if you is shook, you gotta appear unphased make sure motha fuckas know you on all that, at all times. This game full of sharks, if these motha fuckas smell blood they gone close in on it. The only reason I'm here is because I thought you had what it takes to take over Birmingham, if not, move the fuck out the way and let another nigga lead."

"I got what it takes," he affirmed. "You know, you just, Jax. It's hard to get out of that mode."

"I been gone for what, damn near three months now? I ain't yo boss no more, I'm like a co-worker now. "

"Trust me, I'm where I need to be."

"Alright, show me then," I urged as Randal pulled up two black trucks deep as always.

Randal stepped out of his truck with the three men from his truck plus four men from the second truck. The three engines purring and branches crunching underneath their feet were the only sounds as they approached us with the big ass AK's out. I observed Corey's demeanor before I gave my approval because Randal's reputation preceded him, and I needed to make sure this nigga wasn't shook. To the world, Randal was a menacing motha fucka with a long list of bodies. To me he was like a big brother, he always looked out for me, when he found out that Maleek introduced me to the game they got into it because Randal wanted me to be a kid. I was too far gone though and he accepted that, but the close bond he had with Maleek was severed. Randal always told me that Kenneth wouldn't have wanted me in the streets but I wasn't ready to hear it back then, I heard it loud and clear now. The scent of Randal's Cuban cigars wafted through the night air the closer he got to us. I was used to it, I don't think he ever pulled up to a meet without one in the air.

"You finally done dealing with that fuck nigga," Randal questioned me.

"Come on man, please don't start with the *I told you so's*." I laughed.

"You know I am, I always told you that nigga was no good for you. He didn't have your best interests at heart"

"I know, I was blind to the bullshit."

"I hear that pussy is what got you to open your eyes. More specifically, Koda's," he waved his cigar in my direction. The smirk wiped off my face, not because he referred to Koda as pussy because that's just how Randal talked, he didn't mean any disrespect behind it. I was more shocked about how he knew about me and Koda. "You know Koda talked to Simone and I been staying at her crib ever since Maleek thought he could disrespect mine, been waiting to see if he'll come back so I can smoke him legally. Nonetheless, Simone told me y'all took off somewhere together. He was too old to be fucking with her anyways. If she got you to step out the way I love her for you already."

"Yeah man, I tucked that crush for Koda once I found out Maleek was fucking with her. Koda and Simone were like sisters to me, but I guess skipping town like that and being in close proximity to her, I couldn't help it," I shrugged.

"I wouldn't give a fuck if you kicked in his door and stole the bitch out the bed, I'm rocking with you, right or wrong, and that's on Kenneth," he expressed before dapping me up.

"Enough of that personal shit, you gone have to come visit us with Simone one day for the personal shit. Right now we need to focus on this introduction, I got other shit to handle and Koda ain't even feeling me out here right now. Randal this is Corey. He's been running shit since I took off and Maleek got arrested. I helped train him up and he got what it takes to run this shit." I declared with quiet authority.

Randal's eyes assessed Corey in the dim moonlight, and he offered a head nod, recognizing the emergence of a new force in the game.

"Let me ask you this, what are your long-term goals with this shit?"

"Keep my foot on Birmingham's neck. I was trained up by the best and even without the supply, my crew been holding on and keeping them niggas out of our territory. With that raw shit, I know we can make a lot of money together."

"Confident, and these nigga's didn't scare you plus I trust Jax. But I want my money upfront though and no exceptions." Randal nodded, taking a pull from his cigar before exhaling and waving one of his men forward. He passed Corey a prepaid phone before falling back in formation behind Randal. "You'll receive a call on this phone when you can collect your shit. Bring my money in two black duffle bags and it must be nice and neat, I don't have time to fuck around during money exchanges, neat money makes it easier for me to confirm. After we receive our money we'll call one additional time to arrange a pick up of your shipment. You show up, grab your shit, we take the phone and give you a new one then send you on your way. If you fuck up my money one of them will fuck up your entire life."

Randal smiled like he wasn't threatening his life. Corey didn't waiver though, shook his head, body still relaxed. "You don't have to worry about that, shit will go smooth every time."

Randal extended his hand in Corey's direction and the handshake sealed the agreement beneath the dark sky, marking the official transition of power. We retreated to Corey's truck, but before I could shut the door, Randal signaled for me to come over. "Hol' up, I gotta holla at Randal real quick," I stopped Corey from pulling off.

I exited the truck and went to the door that was open for me. Randal was in the car alone and the door closed behind me once I was in the backseat.

"Wassup?"

"Is that the only reason you came back to Birmingham?"

"Now you know I'm not the type of nigga to let a motha fucka have the hand up on me. Koda told me how Maleek ran up in Simone's house looking for her and ever since then I saw a switch in her. She looks over her shoulders, is nervous and shit, even started working from home. Even if I wanted to let the shit be I can't, my lady will sleep better at night when his snake ass is in the dirt.

"You don't have to explain shit to me, some young bulls in Bessemer called and told me they saw him around they way and got his number. Stupid motha fucka didn't think I'd put the word out to the smaller cities too. I guess, like them young niggas out there wouldn't want that bag. Only reason he is still breathing is because I had to meet you here. I can handle it or you can have him if you want."

"That's the last nigga I'mma hit before I disappear. As soon as I left here I was going to find him. I learned from the best."

"Say less."

Randal let his window down and whistled for his men to get in the truck and instructed one of them to inform Corey that he could slide. Corey pulled off as Randal's men claimed their positions in the truck as I got comfortable in the Suburban's seats, it was time. I'd be home snuggling up with Koda watching ESPN while she did sudokus by dinner tomorrow. Thinking of Koda sent guilt through me. I knew she was probably home mad as hell because I left my phone at home with her. Didn't need a phone leaving a digital footprint behind if something went wrong. I knew Koda wouldn't go for that shit and I didn't want to put her too deep in my business, so I left that part of my plan out.

"You really love her huh?"

"On my soul. It wasn't until I came back here that I realized how much Koda was changing a nigga already. Don't laugh but I can be relaxed with Koda. When I'm out of the city, I'm not constantly on edge, checking my surroundings, running down on niggas, and barking orders. I just get to fucking be, cook for her, and meet her for lunch like a regular nigga and shit. She even got me to apply for a cybersecurity analyst program and it starts next week. I don't know if it was Koda alone or a combination of my girl and the sunshine, but being in Florida lifted that dark cloud that follows me. Niggas fear me, but there it was just me, my girl and her parents. They welcomed me with open arms and shit, it really touched a nigga's soul."

"I'm proud as fuck of you. This street shit in me, I love it. I wanted to be in it. You were pushed into this shit before you knew right from wrong for real, and I fell out with my right hand behind this shit so you already know how I feel. When your brother got shot, I held that towel over his chest, applying pressure while Maleek did the dash to the hospital. Kenneth got shot trying to make a play, while he was bleeding out he told us to watch over you and keep you out the streets. We both promised we would, that was his dying wish. I wanted to smoke Maleek back then but you was already too attached to the nigga for me to change your mind, so I let the shit rock. If it wasn't for you, I would've been cut that nigga supply off. When the young boys out in Bessemer called my people about laying eyes on Maleek, he approached one of the youngest niggas out the clique, ready to do him the same way he did you, I know it. He the worst type of nigga. Can't stand on his own, a straight bitch nigga," Randal confessed some shit that he told me when he first found out I was making moves with Maleek, but I wasn't mature enough to receive it back then.

I don't know how I didn't see it, Randal was as solid as they came and I'd always be indebted to him. When I initially planned this trip to Birmingham, I wasn't sure if I'd be able to trust Randal either. If Maleek turned flaw anybody could, but once I was in his presence, I immediately knew I couldn't handle Randal like that. Maleek was a flaw ass nigga from the beginning and it was my fault for overlooking the bullshit.

"That shit means a lot to me, probably more than you'll ever really know."

We sat in silence for another fifteen minutes before we pulled up to a beige house where two young niggas were posted up. I smiled seeing the light skinned nigga with a mouth full of gold teeth that I encountered the night I wiped Madden off the map. Watching him command the respect of the other men and formulate a plan on the spot that night let me know that he was a natural born leader. Stepping out of the car, Randal went to the trunk and retrieved a desert eagle that he placed on his waist while I grabbed an AK-47. He closed the trunk and patted the hood of the truck, signaling for his men to get out of sight.

As we approached the house, Randal made the introductions. "This Speedy and Marlo," he stated, waving at the young light skinned one and a much younger boy who shared the same facial features, he was just dark skinned so I concluded that they were siblings.

"My brother told me what y'all had going on but he can't be involved. I almost knocked his ass out for even being at the liquor store to meet that nigga. Speedy taking his young ass back to school, this ain't for him. He got caught up trying to impress some niggas that I had to handle for thinking they can play with my brother. Ain't that right, Speedy?" Marlo nudged his brother.

"Yeah man," he admitted like he was embarrassed or some shit, staring at the ground and avoiding eye contact. Speedy reminded me of when I was younger and Randal was pushing for me to do better.

"You know who the fuck I am?" I directed at Speedy.

"Fa sho," he nodded.

"Then listen to me, I only say shit once. Your brother said you getting back in school and that's what the fuck you gone do. Unless you want me to be the one to step to you about this shit. Ain't nothing wrong with allowing those who love you to look out for you."

"Respect, I'm getting back in school. You don't have to worry about me," he spluttered.

"Bet," I dapped him up.

"Get up out of here, Ion even wanna hear about you hanging out at a trap house," I commanded.

"But Maleek thinks he's coming to meet me," Speedy argued.

"You said you know who I am so have you ever heard about me repeating myself to niggas?" I responded and he hauled his ambitious ass towards his bike that was laying in the ankle length grass.

"'Preciate you," Marlo nodded and I dapped him up as well before offering a head nod. His phone pinged and he checked the messages while we waited. "This him texting now," he raised his phone, leading the way into the house. "Maleek said he on the way with the cash."

"Tell him to come through," Randal instructed and Marlo tapped away on his phone.

I waited patiently for a nigga I used to love like a brother to arrive so I could snatch his life. How shit can change in only a matter of months. The phone rang when Maleek's bitch ass eased up against the curb in Koda's truck. Bitch ass nigga was too scared to ride around in his own shit. The phone pinged and Marlo read us the message. "He said come grab the cash."

"Tell him to come inside because twelve been circling the block or some shit. If we can finesse him into the spot we can handle this shit right here, if not my men gone cut him off before he can get off the block," Randal explained.

Marlo typed away and I saw the headlights of his whip disappear and the driver's door opened. With a black duffle bag in hand, Maleek approached the house, constantly checking his surroundings. When Maleek finally reached the door, he pulled his gun out, visibly apprehensive about his next move. "Open up lil nigga," he commanded through the door.

In one swift motion, I swung the door open and sent my right fist through his jaw, releasing all of my pent up anger with that first punch, sending him stumbling back. Maleek was about to raise the gun but I swung my other fist, hitting him again before grabbing the gun and placing it up against his head. From the looks of his face, each blow conveyed my level of hurt behind his betrayal. Randal had his desert eagle trained on him as well, and Marlo stepped in, pulling Maleek into the house. I didn't give him a chance to get himself together. I sent my foot to the side of his head before kicking him again in his side.

"Get up bitch ass nigga, you like fighting women and shit! Stand toe to toe with a real nigga," I ordered, kicking him in the side sending blood shooting through his teeth. "If you had hair I'd pull yo ass up by it like you did Koda, pussy!" I spat, kicking him again, trying to put that nigga across the room.

"You lucky I got love for your mama and daddy or else I would've tortured yo ass and left you unrecognizable in the middle of a ditch to send a message. I'mma save them the trouble though, just leave your hands and feet floating in the river or some shit so they can grieve and get over the fact that you're dead."

"You gone do this to me, the nigga that always looked out for you? You can have that bitch man, I ain't tripping. Pussy come a dime a dozen in our life."

"Don't ever address my woman like that," I barked, delivering a kick to his jaw this time. "Pussy being easy for you to come by, is even more of a reason why you should've left her alone before putting your hands on her!"

Reaching for Randal's desert eagle, I couldn't stomach Maleek for a second longer. I couldn't believe I used to look up to this bitch made nigga. Although I was prepared to end this shit, Randal had other plans. Pushing my hand away from his gun, Randal sent two bullets through the middle of Maleek's forehead sending his brains into the wall behind him. "You said the darkness was lifted off you. Let's keep it that way, plus I been wanting to pop this nigga for years," he stated before stepping out of the house and summoning his men.

The truck pulled up, and I hopped inside, giving Randal and Marlo space to chop it up. The men from the second truck went into the house, and brought Maleek's body out shortly afterwards wrapped in a blue tarp. A sudden fire spread through the house and I relaxed in the seat praying that the darkness remained off of me because god damn that shit felt good. Randal hopped in the truck and his driver pulled off.

"After we get you out of those clothes I'll drop you off wherever you want to go."

"My crib, I gotta grab a few things and take my F-150 I left to Simone, so she can handle the transport people for me next week."

"Say less," he commented.

When I got to my condo, Randal waited for me to strip out of my clothes then went to dispose of them while I handled my business. Since he was staying at Simone's spot I planned to drop my truck and keys off over there then get his men to take me to the airport. I quickly showered and gathered the things I wanted to take back to Florida and placed them in a carry-on bag before saying goodbye to my condo. It would be on the market either for sale or a rental by the end of the day. Then it dawned on me, the young bulls could take my spot, it would be better for Speedy to be out the way if we really wanted him to stay out of shit and be great.

Cruising the dark streets under the night sky had me missing the fuck out of Koda. This was the longest I'd went without seeing her since we left Birmingham, and the shit was weird as fuck now. I felt naked, like a piece of me was missing. As soon as I got to Simone's house, I was going to call Koda off her phone until she woke her mad ass up.

Pulling into Simone's driveway, I claimed the empty spot and killed the engine. Approaching the door, I hoped that she was up because Randal hadn't made it back yet. I was apprehensive about waking Simone up, but Georgie's lil annoying ass was barking before I could knock. That lil rappy nigga was loud enough to wake up Simone and her neighbors on both sides. Knocking lightly, her door swung open and I had to blink my eyes twice,making sure that sleep deprivation wasn't playing tricks on me as Koda stood in the doorway, eyes red and puffy from crying.

"The fuck you doing here?" My tone was laced with anger and concern.

She folded her arms across her chest and fought the fresh set of tears that threatened to fall. Wrapping my arms around her, I knew I fucked up. "You left your phone there. I... I... didn't know what to think. Thought maybe you weren't coming back but I didn't want to be in Florida without you."

"Come on man," I scooped Koda off her feet and carried her into the house. She wrapped her arms around my neck and her tears saturated my hoodie. Simone stirred from her slumber and looked up at us.

"I been calling you and Randal, and neither one of y'all answered the phone so I couldn't get your girl to calm down."

"You know we sometimes ditch the phones and get missing, Simone."

"I tried to tell Koda that but she wouldn't listen. Hopped her ass on a plane, had me picking her up in the middle of the night. Now that you're here and you're safe, I'm going to bed, feel free to stay but keep it the fuck down. I'm tired. Come on Georgie," she kissed and he ran in her direction as she locked the door and headed for the stairs.

"I'm tired as fuck. Planned to sleep in the airport while I waited for the next flight into Tampa but you here so I don't have to rush now. Which room you claimed?"

"Upstairs next to Simone, she said her brother and his men were taking up the rooms downstairs," she informed me.

Guiding Koda back onto her feet, I placed my hand on the small of her back, letting her take the lead as we ascended the stairs. Closing the door behind us, I pulled the hoodie over my head then kicked off my shoes and joggers. Koda was already dressed in a long sleeve pajama set. She climbed into the bed and I slid in behind her, pulling her close and planting a kiss on the back of her neck.

"Don't ever do no crazy shit like this again. I love you, I need you, I ain't never gone leave you. Do you know what type of monster I would become if I lost you?"

"I'm sorry," she lamented.

"Ion don't want an apology, I want understanding. If I say some shit, I mean it, I ain't never gone lie to you. You gotta trust in this bond we share as much as I do, Koda."

"I trust you, I just had a weak moment... no, an insecure moment," she sniffled. Turning Koda over, I wiped her tears away before kissing her lips. I just had to feel her heart beating against my chest, feel her breath tickle my throat while I held onto her in this position. God damn she had a nigga's heart.

EPILOGUE

Koda

A Year Later

In the quiet stillness of the morning, the scent of freshly brewed coffee wafted through the air as I sat by the window gazing at the busy city below me. I took a sip of my coffee and allowed the warm sun rays to kiss my skin as I reveled in the moment. Some might think this was fucked up, but I hadn't felt real relief until it was announced that both of Maleek's hands and his right foot were found in a trash bag behind one of his restaurants two months ago. The burden of abusive words and heavy hands had become a distant memory the day that I crossed that line and had sex with Jax.

However, the confirmation of his demise reached me like a soft breeze, carrying with it the unmistaken scent of liberation. Jax never told me what he did during his impromptu trip to Birmingham, but the subtle assurance that I didn't have anything to worry about anymore spoke volumes. We remained in Birmingham for another week after spending the night at Simone's house, and I was able to rehire my team and get Stellar Financial Services back up and running before we went back to Florida. Despite my team having already secured new employment or working independently, persuading them to return was easy. Throughout the relaunch of my business, Jax stood faithfully by my side, assisting with anything I needed.

Just as Jax crossed my mind, I felt his strong hands gently caress my shoulders from behind. I lifted my left hand and placed it on top of Jax's before leaning my head over to kiss his ring finger which displayed our commitment to each other in the form of a wedding ring. Last month we got married in a courthouse ceremony with my parents, Randal, and Simone present.

"Man, don't kiss my ring, that's some hoe shit," Jax stated.

"Boy," I chuckled. "You be ready to ruin the mood."

"I just wanted to make you smile," he laughed. "What you thinking about?"

"How far we've come," I expressed.

We really had come a long way. It was only right that I resigned from my previous position and expanded my business, and Stellar Financial Services now had a second office in Tampa. Jax completed the six months cyber security course, passed the certification exam, and my companies were proud to be his first client and I continued to spread the word to anyone else who would listen.

Even though Maleek and I weren't married, I worked in finance and I wasn't naive. My name graced every document—the trust, life insurance, deed to the properties he owned, power of attorney, and the beneficiary to his bank accounts. That's what led me to Birmingham, I was keeping the money but I didn't want anything to do with the rest of the assets I inherited from Maleek's death. The restaurants weren't my thing, the house we used to share held some of the darkest memories of my life, and I didn't care to be anybody's landlord. Therefore, I met with Maleek's parents at my lawyers office this morning to sign those assets over to them before we left Birmingham this morning.

"And we got a long way to go," Jax leaned down and kissed my lips. "You ready?"

"Absolutely," I beamed, standing from my seat.

Strutting over to the sink of our hotel room, I poured the coffee down the drain as Jax grabbed our suitcase. This was an overnight trip so we packed everything we needed in one large suitcase. Exiting the hotel, we found the valet with our rental car ready and waiting near the entrance. Jax slid the young man a hundred dollar bill before we slipped into the car. Upon reaching the airport, Jax clasped my hand in his left, while pulling our suitcase with his right, guiding us in a direction opposite to our usual path.

"Where are we going?"

"Relax, you know I got you," he assured me.

When we arrived at the private jet terminals opposite the busy commercial terminals, I spotted Simone and Randal seated in one of the private lounges. Since we were only in Birmingham for twenty-four hours I hadn't seen Simone during this trip. I tried to persuade her to meet me for an early breakfast before our flight but she flaked on me at the last minute.

"Did you really think I wasn't going to spend my bestie's birthday with her in Florida or see her before she left Birmingham?" Simone squealed and I looked up at Jax with a bright smile on my face, this had his name written all over it.

Releasing the grip I had on Jax, I rushed over and wrapped Simone up in my arms. We gleefully jumped up and down, causing a scene in the middle of the airport while Jax and Randal looked on. This was the start of an amazing twenty-seventh birthday week.

Flying private was an experience that I definitely wanted to do over and over again. When we made it back to Florida, my parents were geeked to see Simone and Randal, and fed us like a bunch of stuffed pigs before we all went our separate ways.

Waking up this morning, I was excited to see what else Jax had in store for my birthday. He was already out of bed, as usual, and I went to handle my hygiene before meeting Jax in the common areas. The house was flooded with birthday balloons and that didn't shock me because Jax never missed an opportunity to grab balloons and flowers.

"Good morning birthday girl, happy birthday," he greeted me with a smile.

"Thank you," I bubbled, bouncing over to him.

Behind him on the kitchen counter sat some of my favorite breakfast items. Wrapping my arms around Jax, I planted a kiss on his lips and he gripped my neck, intensifying the moment. He spun me around so my back was up against the counter and I eased up there, opening my legs.

"Calm down before you ruin the day," Jax spoke, breaking the kiss.

"What? It's my birthday," I whined as a knock appeared at the door.

"Simone was already on the elevator. Although I wanted you all to my fucking self on an isolated island or some shit, I recognized how selfish that would be. Since we were kids, you and Simone have been inseparable, and now y'all only physically see each other every two or three months. Plus if I would've taken you out of the country your parents would've thrown a fit. They haven't even been able to wish you a happy birthday for the past few years." Jax expressed, repositioning his dick in his basketball shorts before going to open the door. I slid off the counter and took a deep breath.

"Good morning," Simone chirped, entering the condo with Randal right behind her. "Ohhhh this is niceeeee," she bubbled, looking out the windows.

"Thank you, I love it," I admitted.

"She ain't even want to come see the spot at first," Jax called me out.

"I was just so used to living in a house," I stated.

"We can do that too whenever you ready to start looking, for now, y'all gotta eat so I can drop y'all off at the spa."

"Chivalrous and a chauffeur, who knew you had it in you," Simone directed at Jax before going into the kitchen to wash her hands.

"Leave my baby alone," I giggled. "He's all that and more."

"I just never would've thought this is where 2024 would've taken us," Simone stated.

"It did and I ain't going nowhere, so get used to it," Jax assured her.

We sat down and ate breakfast then as Jax stated, he took us to the spa my mother worked at, and we had a relaxing experience. She wasn't there and I'm sure that's because she was getting prepared for my birthday dinner tonight. Spending time with Simone would be the highlight of my birthday week no matter what we did.

After the spa, I was relaxed and the day was almost over. I only had time to go home, get my makeup done, squeeze into my dress, and join those closest to me at Eddie V's. My mom planned an intimate dinner for me, Randal, Simone, Jax, Michelle, Dajana and a few of my employees from the Birmingham and Tampa office that I had a good relationship with, were in attendance.

Scanning the room, I found myself enveloped in pure, unfiltered love. A screen cycled through pictures of me, capturing moments from my birth to just last month when I took Jax to Jamaica for his birthday. The smile plastered on my face narrated my journey—a woman who rose from the ashes of her past, now basking in the radiance of her resilience as a survivor.

Thank you so much for taking the time to read Jax and Koda's story! Make sure you join my mailing list as I'll have exclusive bonus content dropping this year.

https://bit.ly/2RTP3EV

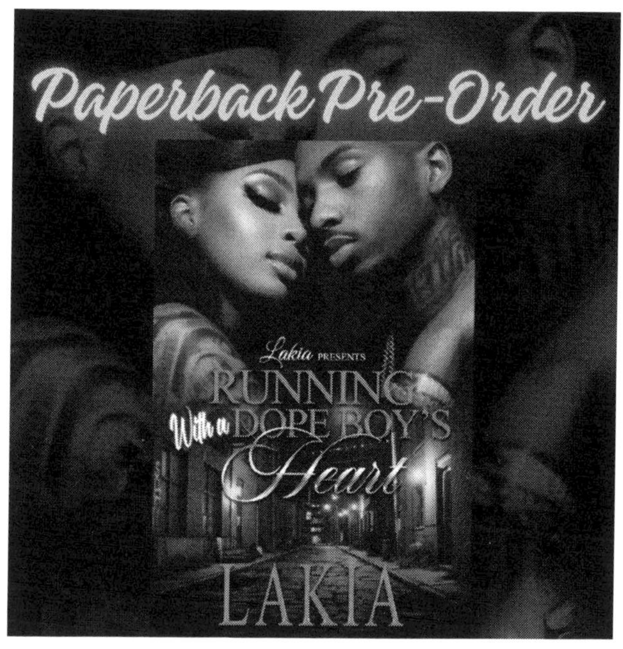

Pre-order your signed paperbacks on my website!
www.authorlakia.com/product/running-with-a-dope-boy-s-heart-pre-order

FOLLOW ME ON SOCIAL MEDIA

Instagram: https://instagram.com/authorlakia
Facebook: https://www.facebook.com/AuthorLakia
Facebook: https://www.facebook.com/kiab90
TikTok: https://www.tiktok.com/@authorlakia

Join me in my Facebook group for giveaways, book discussions and a few laughs and gags! Maybe a few sneak peeks in the future. https://www.facebook.com/groups/keesbookbees
Or search Kee's Book Bees

JOIN AUTHOR LAKIA'S MAILING LIST!

To stay up to date on new releases, contests, and sneak peeks join my mailing list. Subscribers will enjoy the FIRST look at all content from Author Lakia plus exclusive short stories!
https://bit.ly/2RTP3EV

ALSO BY LAKIA

Surviving A Dope Boy: A Hood Love Story (1-3)

When A Savage Is After Your Heart: An Urban Standalone

When A Savage Wants Your Heart: An Urban Standalone

Trapped In A Hood Love Affair (1-2)

Tales From The Hood: Tampa Edition

The Street Legend Who Stole My Heart

My Christmas Bae In Tampa

The Wife of a Miami Boy (1-2)

Fallin For A Gold Mouth Boss

Married To A Gold Mouth Boss

Summertime With A Tampa Thug

From Bae To Wifey (1-2)

Wifed Up By A Miami Millionaire

A Boss For The Holidays: Titus & Burgundy

Miami Hood Dreams (1-2)

A Week With A Kingpin

Something About His Love

Craving A Rich Thug (1-3)

Risking It All For A Rich Thug

Summertime With A Kingpin

Enticed By A Down South Boss

A Gangsta And His Girl (1-2)

Soul Of My Soul 1-2

Wrapped Up With A Kingpin For The Holidays

New Year, New Plug

Caught Up In A Hitta's World

The Rise Of A Gold Mouth Boss

A Cold Summer With My Hitta

Soul Of Fire

Sweet Licks (1-3)

Riding The Storm With A Street King

Running Off On My Baby Daddy At Christmas Time

Crushing On The Plug Next Door (1-2)

Love Headlines

Gone Off His Thug Kisses (1-2)

Saint

Asim

Confessions Of An Ice Princess

Rambo & Gianna: A Very Hood Christmas